Enter to win

Kirsten Jany

Artist: Jimmy Gibbs

Editor: Estela Kennen

Cover Photo by Jovienne Jany

To the girls: Jovienne Jany and Adana Kennen. And to my parents C. & W. Lindgens

Los Angeles Times, April 14, 2013

Director stabbed on set

Burbank, CA. The body of director Rob de Heer was found yesterday on a television set at Skyview Entertainment. He appeared to have been stabbed. The police department did not immediately release whether any suspects had been apprehended. A representative for Skyview Entertainment could not be reached for comment. De Heer, 47, was best known as director of the soap opera *Crystal Falls*, which recently made headlines by urging viewers to send in their real-life stories to be used on the show.

* * * *

Jeremy Lawren – Rob's Assistant

I guess if you find these pages, things aren't looking too good for me. Who knows if I'm still alive? Who knows if anyone will care? After all, I'm just the assistant, and the guy I used to work for is dead already. The police advised me to keep a log, a place for me to observe and tell the truth. If only I knew what that was!

Even if we may never meet, I'd hate to go down as the unknown, faceless, dead assistant. My name is Jeremy Lawren. I am twenty-seven years old and have a Journalism Degree from Georgia State University in Atlanta. I came to LA three years ago. A friend of mine who worked as a cameraman on *Crystal Falls* had invited me. He introduced me to Rob, who was looking for an assistant at the time. I was unemployed, and the thought of working on a television show seemed intriguing. Yep, looking back, I was quite naïve. I ended up as nothing but a chauffeur/courier/babysitter/clean-up boy. Long hours with crappy pay, spent at the bottom of the production totem pole. Rob was a jerk to work for, another truth you will only find here. 'Cause this is Hollywood, and you can't say those things out loud.

He was an incompetent jerk, might I add, always blaming his mistakes on others. He snapped under pressure and treated cast and crew with utter disrespect. My friend, the cameraman, eventually quit. I was debating whether to follow suit. Problem was, I didn't have a job lined up yet. But given the show's steadily declining ratings, I figured I'd better start looking around.

But I have to concede I had underestimated Rob. Say what you will about him, he was a shrewd businessman. We had to stay on air to crank out just enough shows to land that all-important syndication deal. And after weeks in a ratings slump, Rob walked in one day and announced a contest he had dreamed up to generate publicity: So you think your life is a soap opera? While other shows were offering walk-on parts, our contestants were vying for a chance to have a character shaped after them. Plus, there was the small matter of two hundred grand in cash. A nice little incentive to share your pain.

2

I'll admit, I was cynical. Man, did we even have to turn soap operas into reality shows now? Couldn't anybody write a script anymore?

"Aw, lighten up, Jerry," Rob had insisted. "Yeah, we might use their stories. And hey, look at it this way; at least they didn't go through all that crap for nothing!"

I had a bad feeling about it from the start, though for all the wrong reasons. I did not foresee that the contest would ultimately cost Rob his life. The police are convinced the key to Rob's murder lies in the final four contestants. Rob himself had claimed at least one of them wasn't telling the whole story. And then he was found dead shortly after. That's weighed heavily on my mind, because I had picked the entries. The contestants had subsequently been invited to stay in a villa in the Hollywood Hills, provided by one of Rob's friends. Rob was going to crown one of them the winner before he was found brutally stabbed. It didn't happen on the actual set, as the papers wrongly reported, but in one of the adjacent utility closets. And while he still had a large utility knife stuck in his back, an autopsy later revealed the actual cause of death as blunt force trauma to the head, most likely inflicted by the fire extinguisher. Moreover, the two hundred grand had disappeared. Someone, presumably one of the contestants, knew about the safe and the prize money.

Yes, the contestants. Allow me to give you a quick rundown. Trish and Michael are desperate to see themselves on TV and get their fifteen minutes, while Corinne only seems to be in it for the money. The last guy, Stephen, is not the type to hang around a soap set. I'm pretty sure he has never watched the show. In fact, I don't think you could pay him to be here. No, he's got his own reasons. More noble than the rest of us. In light of the tragedy of Rob's death, it seems odd that the contest is still on. But continuing is in the best interest of both the police and the studio. It might be our only shot at solving Rob's murder.

I wasn't there that fatal night. I was at the police station, bailing out my friend, the cameraman. And really, what better alibi can you have? He had gotten into an argument that escalated into a full-blown bar fight. With more than fifteen parties involved, I had spent the better part of the night waiting at the station to post his bail. I was, thus, the first person to be ruled out as a suspect. The police concluded they might as well use me to help in the investigation. The plan is for me to move into the villa where the contestants are staying. I'll be living among them under the guise of shooting a little promo piece about how they landed a part on our show.

Before you ask, yes, I was adequately warned about the dangers. And if I end up dead ...that moron, you might think. Why did he agree to live with the four prime suspects? Maybe that's the journalist in me. Embedded with the enemy troops. But in truth, my motives were far less admirable. It was guilt driving me. One of my contestants had murdered Rob. I had willingly invited the murderer. It was a hard thing to take. Out of all the entries, I had selected these four. Could I have known? That's the question I've been asking myself. I spend my nights going over their submissions, trying to justify why I had picked each one at the time. I remember selecting Corinne, the girl who had spent her entire life below the poverty line. Yeah, two hundred grand must have looked good to her. And she was pretty. One of the few contestants who had included a picture. Her piercing blue eyes struck me, and I selected her based solely on her looks. Call me shallow. What do you expect? I work on a soap—and not a very good one. At first I resented her for manipulating me with her picture. But then I realized she would have that same effect on Rob. He would consider the pick a job well done. Yep, she was exactly what he was looking for when he launched that stupid contest.

* * * *

Corinne Prichett

How many people really know what being poor is like? Sure, statistics say it's a large number. But those of us going through it feel completely alone. At least none of the characters on your show have that problem. You don't see poverty on soaps. Please don't let that stop you from reading my entry.

My name is Corinne. I'm twenty-four years old. Up until eight months ago, I was a check-out girl at a convenience store at the corner of Queen and Peter Street in Toronto. I sold lottery tickets and phone cards and, of course, cigarettes. Until one day it all went up in smoke. Literally. An electrical fire gutted the place. Turned out the owners, Mr. and Mrs. Leung, didn't have insurance. All because the ever-increasing price of cigarettes led to frequent convenience store robberies for smokes, which in turn sent insurance rates through the roof. Add to that the rising costs of electricity and property taxes, and well, the mounting costs of everything under the sun, and it's easy to see why the Leungs were uninsured.

Now a check-out girl doesn't have much in the way of savings. Or furniture. Or clothes. My apartment—really more of a "hole with a washroom"—consisted of a roll-away bed that doubled as a couch, a TV that switched intermittently from picture to no picture to black and white picture, and a small desk that I had picked up from a garage sale and carried home three blocks.

And now my job was gone. I walked to an employment agency in the west end of town the next day. I couldn't afford the subway, definitely not now. Besides, three bucks for a one-way was simply a rip off.

"What kind of sector are you looking for?" the woman the name tag identified as R. White asked, motioning to the chair opposite her desk.

Sector? What sector? Did I look like the kind of person that got to choose a sector? No, I needed work. The kind that would feed me, clothe me, and pay at least six hundred seventy-eight dollars in rent. Provided I'd stay in that hole for a while. And preferably something within walking distance or I'd have to shell out extra bucks for the Metropass.

"I finished high school. My last work was at a convenience store," I informed her. And then it hit me, that was where I'd spent the past three years. I had always assumed it was temporary. Something better would come along. But college was out of the question. There was simply no money.

"Okay, retail," R. White determined. I wondered what jobs she'd had. A small, stout woman in her late forties, she seemed to blend in with the pale off-white furniture in her cubicle. If she had to list her ethnicity in one of those forms they asked you to fill out in the lobby, that's exactly what she'd be: off-white. She could work for years without anyone really noticing she was there. Just a small dent in their payroll. And now this woman was in charge of my future.

"We have an opening in the small appliance section at S____, yes?" She scanned my face for approval of this incredible find. Small appliances. I didn't even own a coffee machine. "I have to warn you though, it involves long hours standing on your feet. But you're young. How old are you?"

"Twenty-four." Great. My only job qualifications were that I was twenty-four and could stand on my feet. R. White gave me the once-over. Would I have to stand up now to show her I could do it?

"Maybe there's something else," she said in a more hushed tone. Now this sounded special. Big appliances? The kind I had to save my quarters for once a week? "Here." She pulled out the secret file from under her desk. "This just came in this morning. Ever worked in a health spa?"

A spa? Did this woman have the faintest idea how broke I was? Spa days weren't exactly on my list. But judging by her mousy appearance, R. White didn't blow her money on personal indulgences either. I was pretty sure neither one of us had ever seen the inside of a spa. The job posting was for a receptionist. Someone outgoing and energetic who would work well within their team.

"Is there..." I hesitated, but realized I had no choice, "Is there a dress code?"

R. White looked at me, and for the first time I saw her as an accomplice.

"Not officially." She leaned over her desk, her voice falling back into the hush. "But... you know those places... it's very upscale, so appearance is important, of course."

I nodded, defeated.

"Here." R. White reached into her magic box under the desk again, this time pulling out a business card. "They can help you."

First Impressions – Quality Clothing for the Workplace
A Charitable Organization

First Impressions was within walking distance. So far, so good. A woman named Anna was in charge of making me presentable. To be fair, I gave her enough to work with. Not that I'm arrogant. But I'm thin and have shoulder-length brown hair that she deemed would look most sophisticated in a simple updo. I walked out with a dark grey pair of pants, a simple white blouse, and instructions on how to recreate the updo. I'd have to invest in a pair of shoes. After all, I couldn't show up in my grocery store sneakers. Something sensible, durable. Nothing flashy or people would notice I was wearing the same pair every day.

The morning of the job interview was sunny. Good thing I wouldn't have to show up in my coat. The spa was in the north end. If I got up an hour early, I could walk there. By winter I'd be forced to get a Metropass.

I checked myself over in the store windows, pleased you couldn't tell I was poor and desperate. None of their business, anyway. I silently debated whether to splurge on a cappuccino. No, I'd wait 'til I got closer to the place so I could walk in with a coffee. I'd look more relaxed, more in control. Like the kind of person that could afford the Starbucks addiction.

I slowed my steps, trying not to get to Bloor Street too early. Walking by the newspaper boxes, I glanced at the headlines. Another fiery crash on the 401. I bent down to look at the grisly picture when something caught my eye. It was golden and sparkly and lying at the foot of the paper box. For a moment I thought it couldn't be real. An engagement ring. I picked it up, slid it into the pocket of my charity pants, and walked on. I stared straight ahead for several blocks until I was sure nobody had noticed. Nobody was following me, nobody looking. I pulled the ring out in front of a furniture store display and slipped it on. Perfect fit. Like it was made for me. It was breathtaking. The most precious thing I had ever seen, let alone touched. For a few moments I must have just stared at it sparkling on my finger. When I looked up, a woman beside me was smiling ear to ear.

"Congratulations!"

And that was the moment my life turned into one gigantic lie. The store window no longer reflected someone at the bottom of the social ladder. No, this young woman had it all: the clothes, the friends, the wealthy fiancé. She was going places. She wasn't looking for a job, but a new opportunity. And by the time I reached my destination, I had almost convinced myself.

The spa was just off Bloor Street. I had checked out their website at the local library the night before. The place used to be called Morgandale's, after the owners Morgan and Dale Groot. They had recently undergone some changes and now called themselves "The Pulse—Your Complete Wellness and Beauty Centre." Trendy. They offered everything from manicures to botanical detoxification and holistic reflexology, none of which I got a chance to google. My time was up, and some old guy bumped me off the computer. Now here I was at that all-important first interview, ignorant.

Nobody noticed me enter. For a few moments I just stood there, twisting the ring on my finger. They definitely needed a receptionist. Someone to acknowledge the customers when they walked in. Nobody should feel as lost as I did just then.

"Oh, hi." A precariously thin blonde stepped out of the shadows. "I'm sorry, have you been waiting long, Miss? Do you have an appointment?" She reached for the thick leather-bound book behind the counter, obviously mistaking me for someone who could afford this place.

"I'm here for the job interview." I somehow managed to sound confident. Must have been my new hand-me-down career pants rubbing off. "The receptionist job you're trying to fill."

"Oh, yes, right, right. Then you must be…" She glanced back at the book, "…Corinne. I'm Morgan." She held out her hand and smiled, exposing two rows of professionally whitened teeth that somehow seemed too big for her mouth.

"My partner and I have been expecting you." That seemed rather pompous considering her business partner was her sister. And they quite evidently had forgotten about the interview.

She motioned for me to follow her through the tastefully lit salon, the "Skin Care Lounge and Beauty Consultation Centre," as she pointed out in passing. She led me to a small office in the back, where her sister—and business partner—was on the phone ordering supplies. The two couldn't have been more different. Both well into their fifties, neither one of them seemed to belong in a Wellness Centre. I had to suppress an urge to force-feed Morgan, whose bony cheekbones protruded dangerously, threatening to break her paper-thin skin. The countless wrinkles around her mouth reminded me of discarded Christmas wrapping paper, all scrunched up. Who on earth would buy those overpriced bottles in the foyer display from this lady, thinking she had hit upon the fountain of youth? Dale, on the other hand, a little on the heavier set side, looked like she belonged in a Gypsy bazaar selling home-made pottery. Sporting three different hair colors from dark red to two shades of orange, she made me second-guess my decision to go with a mere rose lip gloss.

"Have a seat, dear," Morgan said, inviting and condescending at the same time. "Corinne is here for the job interview. Tell us a bit about yourself, would you, dear?"

Despite the butterflies in my stomach, I managed to put on a pretty good show. I mentioned my retail experience, my organizational skills, my ability to multitask, work within a team while needing little supervision, and everything else they could have possibly wanted to hear. I even faked actively maintaining a healthy lifestyle and thriving in a customer-service-related environment. Truth is, I'm a loner. Always have been. Partly because I like it that way. Partly because I never had any money to go anywhere. It was just easier to hang out at home, and library books were free.

After about fifteen minutes I figured the sisters were reasonably impressed. Morgan flashed her big white fangs at me while Dale nodded at whatever I had just said.

"I like your style," Morgan said, smiling generously, "the way you carry yourself. I like your understated sense of fashion. Very mature for your age. I think it fits our clientele. Not that you can ever voice this out loud, but appearance is a big part, you know." I did know. R. White had already beaten her to the punch. "The way some of the applicants show up here, the big evening makeup, the overbearing jewelry... But you just kept it to one classy piece. May I see that, dear?" Without waiting for a reply, she reached for my left hand. A clear breach of the employment code. You do not touch the applicant. Or call them 'dear'.

"What an incredibly beautiful ring," she gushed. "So you're engaged?"

"Yes," I said. Wow, without a moment's hesitation. She was not allowed to ask me that, anyway. She deserved a false answer.

"My, my." She giggled. "Judging by the size of that rock, I'd say he's a keeper."

"Morgan," her sister admonished, shaking her red and orange head. "You've got to excuse my sister. She gets a bit carried away sometimes."

"That's okay." I smiled back. "I'm very happy with my fiancé, thank you. His name is Brett. He works for a large investment company over on Bay Street."

"That sounds wonderful. We'd love to meet him some time. And," Morgan glanced over at her sister, who nodded, "I think we both agree, you seem like the exact candidate we were hoping for."

Jeremy Lawren

The second entry I picked was the one I'd most likely get flagged for. An accused murderer. Yeah, I know what you're thinking. In my defense, Michael had been acquitted by a jury. At the time, that was good enough for me.

Besides, the person he had been accused of murdering was his late wife. So it was really more of a domestic case. This wasn't some random killer. I wasn't so stupid as to endanger any one of us, believe me. Then again, you can never spot a killer. We should all know that by now. Turn on the TV. It's always the quiet guy down the road. And he always waves and says hi.

So why did I pick Michael? His story was just sensational—and controversial—enough to appeal to Rob (which proved right). Honestly, finding suitable material among the entries wasn't easy. The viewers that sent in videos apparently didn't feel the need to rehearse before going on camera. And the ones that bothered writing their stories out didn't do much better. Though we received bags full of mail, they weren't the kind of stories that would revive our show. Two-thirds of our audience were disgruntled housewives, dragging out their petty feuds. One woman was convinced a neighbor had tapped her phone. There was also no shortage of sarcastic entries, clowns obviously mocking our show. They had either been abducted by aliens or couldn't recall their stories due to amnesia. I counted fifteen entries signed "Bobby Ewing."

Then I came across Michael's submission, and I must admit I was intrigued. This was either some poor soul who not only had to cope with his wife's death, but some incredible accusations—or a cold-blooded killer. There was no in-between. I was curious to meet him. Would I be able to tell face to face?

Well, I was in for a surprise. Michael was nothing like I had pictured him. Seriously, I was taken aback by how arrogant and condescending this jerk was. Call me crazy, but I thought the guy owed me for getting him here. Yes, his was the entry I regretted picking most.

* * * *

Michael Palmer

I'm sure you've received stacks of submissions, but I doubt anyone has gone through what I have. No, I'm not looking for fame or fortune, though there was a time when two hundred grand would have meant the world. Now I just want to clear my name, something that should have happened once the case against me had been dismissed. But for the public, my neighbors, my former friends I remained a *persona non grata*.

I'm guilty of many things. But killing my wife is not one of them. A failure in business, a lousy husband, an ungrateful son-in-law, all true. But not a cold-blooded killer. I could never do that, let alone to someone I loved. And though I did nothing to save my marriage, I did love her.

My name is Michael. I am forty-five years old and now live in Waltham, just outside Boston. I moved here from Cambridge, though the move did nothing to help. Of course nobody here believes me either, and you can only live like this for so long. That half-second hesitation in their eyes—should they greet me?—never passes. My paper is never on my doorstep. Not even the paper boy wants to get too close to the guy who maybe/possibly/surely killed his wife and got away with it. Except, I didn't. I didn't kill her, and I have yet to get away.

A few weeks before my wife died, we had a huge fight. Granted, we had many of those. But this particular Friday night sticks in my mind. Maybe because it signified the beginning of the end. Maybe because I wasn't expecting a fight that day. I stupidly thought things were getting better. Not surprisingly, we were arguing about my father-in-law who had been recently admitted to a nursing home. Alzheimers had turned him into an unpredictable old child, wavering between outbursts, unreasonableness, and sheer apathy. We simply couldn't keep him with us any longer. A home seemed the only option. But he wasn't adjusting well and had swallowed some of his roommate's blood pressure pills he had swiped from the nurse's cart in an unsupervised moment. Nothing major happened. He ended up feeling nauseous, but fortunately that remained the extent of the damage. The director of the home apologized profusely and promised to review prescription safety procedures with all his staff. Still, Karen was livid.

"How could this happen?" she fumed. "See, I told you this wouldn't work. He's only gone two days and already this. These guys were supposed to watch him!"

I resisted the urge to point out it could have happened to anyone. In fact, it did happen to us once. A bottle of Aspirin left on the counter nearly turned into a fatal event. Karen herself had forgotten to put the pills away. But I knew better than to bring it up right then.

I tried to calm her down. "Look, he's gonna be fine. They caught it right away. I'm sure from now on they're gonna be extra careful with him."

"I don't know. I just don't trust the place after this." Karen rinsed out the coffee mug I had left on the breakfast counter, turning the tap on full blast. An angry gush of water sprayed through the air. "Besides, it feels like we're putting him out to pasture."

I was annoyed we were, yet again, talking about her dad. For the past three years, we had talked about little else. It was the only thing left to talk about. Now he had taken merely two days to do something stupid again.

"He'll be fine," I repeated tiredly.

"That's easy for you to say. You don't care." She forcefully opened the kitchen cupboards and plunked the mug down.

"Of course I care," I insisted.

"Besides, he doesn't know his way around Fall River. Why did Julian have to move him that far away?"

"It's not that far away. It's an hour's drive."

"Whatever." She blew some stray hair out of her face. Her hair was always in a ponytail these days. She used to wear it loose. "What if he wanders off? He'll get lost and won't find his way back."

"I'm sure the nursing staff will keep an eye on him. Especially now."

"You really don't care."

"I do care." Our fights always started out like this. We'd be talking about her dad, then get into yet another argument. "I've put up with him for the past three years. Does that sound like I don't care?"

"Put up with him? So that's how you see it. Nice to know that you care that much. I'll tell you what, as soon as I get my lawyer to draw up those papers, you won't have to put up with any of us anymore. You're free to go." She stormed off down the hallway, then the bedroom door slammed. Did she actually have a lawyer or was it just a bluff? Ah well, another night on the couch.

I grabbed a beer from the fridge and sank onto the leather love seat. I could hear the tinkling of the wind chimes on our balcony. Karen must have untied them. I had lost count how many times I had taped them together. How could she describe that as a "soothing" sound? I hated it. Like something straight out of a horror movie. Maybe this wasn't so different from a horror movie after all. My business had gone down the tubes, and now my marriage was failing. Two for two. How much worse could it get? The last five years had been one uphill battle. Now I'd be forced to close down the graphics design company I had run with my brother-in-law Julian for many years. We'd have to clear out the office by the end of the month.

We used to do well, Julian and I. Trade show logos, corporate designs, direct mail. Not outrageously well, but steady work. But slowly things changed. People's home offices had gotten more sophisticated, and so had their printers. Savvy college students could compete at much lower rates. Even the local printing shops were offering cheap in-house graphics. Julian saw it coming. But I stuck my head in the sand. Where would I go from here? Already in my forties, I would have trouble finding work. I'd have to start over, make a name for myself. Doing what exactly? I couldn't tell.

I took another sip of beer. Of course she was concerned about her dad. But we simply couldn't keep him with us any longer. Couldn't she see that? We had essentially become prisoners in our own place. We had to hide all the cleaning supplies. We had to make sure he wouldn't be anywhere near the oven. The medicine cabinet had to be locked at all times. At night we'd have to get up repeatedly to check he was still in his room. The smallest sound made Karen shoot out of bed.

Her brother Julian had finally stepped in. "You're running yourself ragged, Karen. You've got to let him go. You can't keep caring for him around the clock. The people at the nursing home are much better equipped for that. And let's face it, it's going to get worse. He's gonna need more and more care."

I had told her that for months, but she wouldn't listen. She had stopped listening to me a long time ago. Julian finally put his foot down. He arranged the move to the nursing home and the transfer of my father-in-law's care to a new doctor. Yes, I was grateful the day my father-in-law finally moved out. Did he really have to lodge with us for free all that time? Finally one less mouth to feed. My suspicions proved right. He must have pocketed some money from the sale of his house way back when. Enough to cover the nursing home care, which neither Julian nor we could have afforded. Karen's dad could have easily contributed something while living with us. But that was never up for discussion. And who was I to complain, when I was living off my wife's teaching job? My eyes wandered around the living room. How much longer could we afford this place? We were three months behind in our condo fees. I finally put the empty bottle down and dialed Julian.

"Hey, it's me. Karen is still throwing a fit."

"Give her some time," he said. "That was certainly enough excitement for his first week there. But I'm sure it won't happen again. They were awfully sorry about the whole thing."

"I know. It's just, she wishes you'd put Dad up somewhere closer to home. Karen would prefer if he was somewhere right around the block."

"I'm sure she would." Julian laughed softly. "And she would be there every hour, every day. And so would you. Excuse me for trying to preserve everyone's sanity."

"I know, I know," I said quickly, trying not to come off as ungrateful.

"Listen, I didn't just pick any ol' place," Julian pointed out. "This home came highly recommended. And I'm sure they'll do fine from now on."

"Yeah, well, try telling that to Karen." I sighed, then grabbed another beer from the fridge.

"Of course she's upset now. We all were. But if it doesn't work out, I promise I'll pick Dad up and bring him back home. All I'm asking is that we give this a try."

Right. But she was ready to file for divorce. That was the problem. Karen didn't want to try anymore.

* * * *

Jeremy Lawren

Ten decent stories from our viewers. Shouldn't be that hard, right? I would present them to Rob, who would then pick the winner. After two days of reading entries, it dawned on me that this would not be that easy. People seemed to equate "soap story" with getting dumped or cheated on, and I almost threw out Trish's story because of that. Not another divorcee. Half of all marriages ended in court anyway. Was this another "I think he tapped my phone" or "I got screwed in the settlement"? It wasn't until she mentioned landing her husband in jail that she caught my attention. Yep, this was definitely one for Rob's files. Sadly though, kids were involved. Kids who had already gone through a divorce and their father's imprisonment. Did they really need this dragged out in front of America's TV viewing public? Man, if this was my mom, I'd be mortified. Rob, of course, didn't care. And I'm sorry to say I cared more about pleasing Rob than following my gut.

* * * *

Trish Grady

Let me start by telling you I'm a huge fan of your show! Never miss an episode! I was so excited to hear about your contest, and I'm thrilled to be able to share my story with you. You want to know what makes my life a soap opera? Certainly not that I'm a single mom, at thirty-nine living in Berwyn, Illinois, with my parents. Or that I'm divorced from my children's father. Plenty of people will go through that. But few ex-wives will get a chance to land their husbands in jail. I can't tell you what that's like, that bittersweet feeling. Part of you wants revenge. But part of you can't comprehend the magnitude of the betrayal. My husband was a criminal. How could someone you once thought you loved be capable of something so horrific?

To the police I was the only eyewitness, a "person of interest." Even that was something new to me. Up to that point, I'd been a person of no interest. Little more than the one who cooked, cleaned, chauffeured her kids around, and somehow got on everybody's nerves. The verbal reminder of chores and appointments. A nuisance no more welcome than the six-thirty alarm that went off in our house every morning.

I had known for a while that Bill was cheating on me. Maybe it was my sixth sense. Maybe it was the fact that we had two cars all of a sudden. Bill was prudent with money. He worked an exact 2.7 miles from home, at R_ Bank where he'd been employed since his early twenties. One car was all we ever needed. I would drive him to work on my way to dropping the kids off at the bus station. And I would pick him up at 5.15 sharp. But then things changed. Bill had been recently promoted to loans officer, and I hardly saw him anymore. Lots of overtime. After-hours meetings to secure mortgages at clients' homes. All part of the game, he explained. He needed his own car. Customer service always comes first. Why didn't the bank provide the car then? It didn't work that way, he scoffed, clearly not willing to discuss it further. I evidently knew nothing about business. Maybe so. I also failed to see why he needed a new cell phone, which I didn't have the number for. He became adamant about separating personal and business calls. If I needed to get a hold of him, I was to leave a message with his secretary. I quickly found leaving messages was pointless. He either wouldn't return my calls, or insist that whatever I had been calling about clearly could wait 'til dinner. The only problem was, he wouldn't make it home for dinner either.

Bill essentially wasn't part of our family anymore. He had quietly checked out. It hit me one morning with glaring clarity after a particularly unpleasant telephone conversation with our local city planning authority. We had recently moved to Cicero, where we had bought a beautiful new three-story townhouse, backing onto a nature preserve. At least that's what we thought. The builder had assured us the adjacent land would remain vacant and forested. But six months after we moved in, construction started. And not just any construction, but a monster twelve-story high-rise. We would be looking out onto their parking lot! And they would be peeking down into our living room!

I'd spent the past twenty minutes complaining to some guy at City Hall—plus an additional ten trying to get through to the right department. To no avail. City council had publicized their meetings about adjustments to the zoning bylaws. I should have voiced my concerns back then. But who on earth reads those tiny little notices in their local paper? A twelve-story building deserved a much bigger notice, in my opinion, as I had pointed out to Bill the night before. "Trish, it's pointless to argue with City Hall," he'd insisted when I had informed him about my intent to complain. "It was preceded by a public announcement. That's all they're gonna say."

And now Bob, the voice from City Hall—if that was his real name—had cited exactly that excuse, and I felt betrayed. Betrayed by our builder, betrayed by the local authorities, betrayed by my husband who had somehow seen this feeble explanation as a valid point and was refusing to join in my fight against City Hall. He didn't care. Of course he didn't. He was never around, anyway. Neither was my thirteen-year-old daughter Megan, who had spent the last week sleeping over at a friend's house after a falling out about her cell phone charges. I was simply uncool and out of touch with the way of the world. Not so. I was most definitely in touch— I got the whole picture from my cell phone bill!

I was debating whether to make an appointment for the hairdresser's, which usually cheered me up. But not anymore. Why bother? Bill wouldn't notice my hair. I was in a rut. My life needed some highlights, not just my hair.

Did I become boring on a particular day or turn insignificant in the process of time? If you're a stay-at-home mom for thirteen years, you just run out of interesting material to contribute at dinner time. Funny, 'cause when you grow up, they put all these big dreams in your head. You think life is all about having a career and turning into someone important. Nope, in reality you will spend most of your life just serving people. Preparing family meals, driving your son to soccer practice and your daughter to the math tutor. Signing field trip permission slips in the car...someone always demanding your attention. Life was nothing but a big tamagotchi.

It dawned on me that I didn't even have any friends. Real friends, that is. People I had chosen to be friends with. Not just the mothers of my children's classmates, forced on me via car pools and school volunteer work. And honestly, who wants to be on the Parent Council Board? I was envious of my thirteen-year-old. She got to pick her friends. Friends whose company she evidently preferred to living with her uptight mother.

"When is Megan coming home?" My eight-year-old son Bryce looked at me. "I want to get on her computer."

"She's still at Olivia's."

"Can I use her computer then?"

"Not without asking her first." I sighed. With Megan gone and Bill hardly home, my family had shrunk down to two.

"It's no fair," Bryce whined. "How am I supposed to ask if she isn't here?"

Perhaps he was on to something. The thought of her little brother using her computer in her absence might send my thirteen-year-old scurrying back home. "Maybe we can call her," I suggested. I was about to pick up the receiver when the phone rang.

"Hello?"

"Mrs. Grady? This is Christy from Dynamo Fitness. Your husband left his wallet here."

"What?"

"His wallet. Your husband left it here last night. Would you like to pick it up? Or do you want me to hold it for him?"

20

I was stunned. He'd said nothing about joining a fitness club. Sure, many people work out. But wasn't it the kind of thing you would mention to your spouse? And how did he find time for the gym when there was none for his family?

"I'll... I think I'll come by and get it. Where are you located again?" She gave me an address just off Main Street. I ordered my resistant eight-year-old into the van and drove off.

Why was Bill working out all of a sudden? We had no family time as it was. Besides, he had mentioned visiting a client last night. Did he go to work out after? No wonder he never made it home for dinner.

Bill seemed evasive when I confronted him that night. "I retrieved your wallet, in case you've been looking for it."

"What?" He barely looked up from the paper, the same one he'd been reading that morning. Gone were the days when we read the paper together. He used to tease me because I always went straight for the obituaries, scanning for any familiar names. It was part of living in a community. I liked to know what was going on. Except, these days I didn't even know what was going on in my own house.

"Your wallet," I said, doing my best to stay calm. "I picked it up from the gym, where you left it. The girl called me this afternoon."

"Ah, good." He turned back to the sports section. The nerve.

"You never told me you signed up for the gym," I countered, my voice shrill.

He shrugged. "I thought I did."

"No, you didn't."

"Trish, keep your voice down or Bryce will wake up."

I took a deep breath, trying to regain my cool. My voice always turned shrill when I got upset. I hated that. I wasn't the controlling nag he made me out to be. I'd simply found it strange that he hadn't told me he had started working out. "So why did you keep it a secret?"

He finally put the paper down. "I wasn't trying to keep it a secret. I thought I told you. I talk to people all day. I can't remember who I've told what."

Liar. "So you'd have no problem with me signing up, too?" I gave him the cold stare.

"Of course not."

"And we could go work out together?"

"No, we'd most likely be going separately. You'd be going during the day, right? And I'd be going after work. We can't leave Bryce alone, and Megan doesn't seem to live here anymore."

Smooth. Pointless to argue with. Besides, I had already spent too much time arguing with him. That's why he barely talked to me now.

"What's with all the suspicion anyway?" He smiled magnanimously. His banker's you've-been-approved smile. "Trish, honey, you just watch too much TV." Well, what else was I supposed to do? It's not like we spent much time together anymore. For the last couple of years, he hadn't even taken me to his bank's Christmas party. He had insisted he wasn't going either, then ended up staying anyway. His coworkers had talked him into it. And nobody seemed to notice I wasn't there. A person of no interest. Up until November 22.

* * * *

Jeremy Lawren

When I picked Stephen, I really just did it to fill my quota. I never thought Rob would go for it. Stephen simply didn't fit. Way too working class. And not the right setting for our show. He worked in a warehouse, or something like that. It was just not glamorous or, depending on your point of view, cheesy enough for *Crystal Falls*. How would we ever incorporate that into the story line? I have to say though, major props to the guy for being the only contestant to openly admit he'd never seen our show. Not one episode. Yep, he had my respect right there.

Stephen had recently lost his wife, who was an avid fan of our soap. He had watched her lose her battle with cancer, and now was trying not to drink. Finally somebody with a goal other than money or fame. Even if he wasn't all that successful at the "not drinking" part, as I later found out. Then again, none of my contestants were quite like they seemed on paper.

* * * *

Stephen Dowell

I have no idea what would make someone's life a soap story. Really, I don't watch soaps. So bear with me if I'm not up to speed on your production. My wife loved your show though. That's why I have to try, for her. Honestly, I don't need to see myself played out on TV. And I don't even care about the money. But it's the least I can do for her now.

My name is Stephen. I'm thirty-eight years old, and I work as an overnight stocker at H____, a large building supplies chain. Probably not good material for a soap. I guess actors prefer to play lawyers or fashion house executives, or lawyers working for fashion house executives. Irene would've known. But no such luck. I can only offer you building supplies and my own little business, home renovations, which I run on the side. Licensed, bonded, insured. Nothing under the table 'cause I'm an honest guy. At least, that's what I thought.

Is that enough "personal info?" What else? I have spent the past fifteen years living in Groton, Connecticut. I'm Scottish by birth, but do you really need to know that? I'm a widower. My wife Irene died four months ago of ovarian cancer. Probably not such good material for a soap either. I understand on TV people have car accidents and get amnesia. Not painfully draining battles with cancer. That's okay; nobody wants to deal with that. I didn't want to either. I totally failed her. But I won't fail her now. As much as I want to drink, I won't because I promised her I wouldn't. It's just hard, trying not to drink and giving up smoking at the same time. I'm sorry if I sound incoherent. I'm a little edgy. Not that I was ever an alcoholic, but Irene worried. She was always concerned about me. I really didn't deserve her. She'd have breakfast ready when I came home in the morning. She'd make sure I'd go for my yearly check-ups, and file my income taxes on time. She took care of all the little things, too. Parking tickets, new work boots, returning phone calls. I could always depend on her. I wasn't used to having someone care for me that much. I'd been on my own since I was sixteen. Never expected anyone to do anything for me. And how did I repay her? I caught myself in a lie. Pretended she never existed. Yeah, I know it's despicable. I have no excuse.

I guess I should've watched your show every now and then, just out of courtesy. My wife was on your mailing list. That's how I know about the contest. I can't bring myself to take her off that stupid list. And I can't bring myself to watch your show now that she's gone. Really sorry. It's all because of that wig. You see, Irene lost her hair during the chemotherapy and went to buy a wig. I thought she'd come home with something short and blond. Something like her old hairstyle. But she didn't. Instead, she had ordered the exact hairdo from one of your characters. Some woman named Ivy, I believe. Shoulder length and reddish—does that sound like someone from your show? Anyway, I could never really get used to it. In some weird way the wig brought back the old Irene, that light in her eyes. She even started to wear make-up again. But in some awkward and sad way, it made her someone else. And I didn't want to remember her like some stupid soap star. No, Irene was so much better than that.

Honestly, I only cried once, and I remember the day. The funeral home had asked me to drop off the dress she would be buried in. For over an hour I just stood in front of her closet. I finally picked something summery and cream colored. The dress was expensive and somewhat of an impulse buy. Irene had debated for days whether she should return it. Would she even have an occasion for it? Now she would. The thought was too much, and I sank down onto the bed, dress still in hand. I placed it beside me and sobbed uncontrollably into one of her prized throw pillows. Now there was finally a use for those.

The wig, I suddenly thought. What about the wig? Should she be wearing it? It wouldn't look like my Irene. But she had lost all her hair so it wouldn't look like her without it either. And she wouldn't have wanted to be buried without hair. The wig made her feel special. Something I should have made her feel. Over and over I played it in my mind. All those things I should've done. I was disgusted with myself. Disgusted to the point it made me nauseous. Nauseous and wanting to drink myself into a stupor. But that would have been the easy way out. And I didn't deserve that. So I forced myself back up and headed to work. 'Cause as long as I worked, I wouldn't be drinking.

The warehouse was hot. The sweat dripped down my back. They turned the air conditioning off at night. The place was an oven. And Thursdays were "door nights" with plenty of unloading to do. We were working with a skeleton crew, only four of us guys. The college kids call in sick Thursdays. Too much heavy lifting and not enough pay to miss a pub night. Somewhat unfair, anyway, us guys getting paid the same as the women. They don't drive any of the equipment and just sit there, ripping open the boxes. H___ needed more manpower. The last three job fairs had netted two guys, one of which quit after the first night. You gotta unload. The trucks have to leave in the morning. You gotta bring the materials in. There's no other room for storage, you know. But people don't get that. If you're shopping in a warehouse store and they're out, well, guess what, they're out! Don't ask "Could you check in your warehouse?" This IS the warehouse!

The supervisor, a woman the college kids referred to as Monstercheeks, yelled. She was coming down on the girls in the barbecue isle. I guess she didn't like the way they'd hung up the utensils. "Don't leave too much of the backboard showing!"

I worked seven nights a week. I used to do five, but I didn't trust myself to be home alone. Breakfast now meant coffee at a diner. I planned my days carefully. Always on the move. Come and go. Just don't stay home too long.

The mail was piling up on my dining room table. One of these days I'd get to all that. I was tired. But I didn't want to lie down. I was still avoiding Irene's dress on my bed. Another message from the funeral home. They really needed me to drop the burial clothes off by tomorrow. And I still didn't know what to do about that wig.

I took a quick shower and jumped back into my truck. I kept driving until I saw the New Haven city sign. Why had I come here? What was I gonna say?

I pulled up in front of the little store, still hesitating. But I owed that sweet, kind lady who had made my Irene feel so special a thank you. I stared at the wigs in the store display, all the while playing with the cigarette lighter in my pocket. Wigs made me uncomfortable. Maybe that's a guy thing. But I definitely felt I didn't belong there. The store bell rang as I walked in. Someone hurried out from the back. This was a bad idea. Maybe I should just leave.

"Can I help you with anything?" a petite redhead asked warmly. She had beautiful, kind eyes. Irene had said she looked like a movie star. But her warmth stood out for me most. Even in those first few seconds. It reminded me of Irene herself.

"Ehm, I was just… just takin' a look around," I stammered.

"Sure, take all the time you want. Are you looking for yourself?"

"No, no." I self-consciously ran a hand through my hair. Why would she assume I'd need a wig? Right, I was in a wig shop. "Actually, I'm just checking around for my mother." My mother?! My mother passed away when I was twelve. What on earth made me say that?

"Well," she said, "picking out a wig for someone else is very difficult. They have to be fitted properly. But if you bring your mother by, I'd be more than happy to sit down with her for a consultation."

Lady, you're twenty-six years too late. Nonsense, my mother died of meningitis. She never needed a wig for that.

"She's a little embarrassed to come down here herself," I continued lying. "After losing her hair, and all."

"A lot of my clients feel that way," the kind lady continued. "But I assure you, there's no need to be ashamed. I try my best to make everybody feel comfortable." I knew that. You did a stellar job with Irene. I was the one that completely let her down.

* * * *

Corinne Prichett

Besides me, *The Pulse* employed four full-time girls, plus two part-timers. My favorite of those was Jenny. She was the hair extensions specialist with endless stories about her ne'er-do-well boyfriend. Unfortunately, she only came in twice a week.

The other girls were nice enough, but I kept my distance. I couldn't squander my money going out with them. After all, I had to invest in some professional attire. First Impressions Anna had given me a few loaners, due back after my second paycheck. The job paid thirteen bucks an hour. Tough enough to live off that. Thankfully Brett, my fictitious fiancé, covered most of our bills. Right.

My work wasn't glamorous, but I enjoyed it: answering phones, restocking supplies, sweeping the floors, and chatting up clients in hopes of selling the latest botanical line with a ten percent commission. I was actually quite good at that. Strategically placed at the reception desk, I knew how to talk our customers into some last minute must-have on the way out. I outsold the entire staff. I blamed the engagement ring, a constant conversational centerpiece. It somehow gave me credibility: my skin looked so good, it had landed me the most swell guy! It, undeniably, added glamour to my folding the towels.

"We're all going to the Metropolis tonight," Jenny said, casually tossing an apple core into the trash. "Jazz works there as a bouncer. First job he's had in... let's see... ten months. First job he's held for a whole week since... ever! Best thing, I can get us in free!"

As tempting as that sounded, I would still have to buy at least two drinks. Plus an outfit.

"Sorry, I can't. We're having dinner with Brett's boss tonight. He says his wife is a gourmet chef."

I hated lying. Especially to Jenny. I kept telling myself soon this whole charade would be over. Eventually, Brett and I would break up. An amicable split, of course. I would sell the ring—or, in the official version, "give it back"—and finally treat my place to some furniture.

At times I thought about the woman who had lost the engagement ring. Did she admit it to her fiancé? Did it cause a

28

fight? Maybe break off the whole engagement? Then again, if he broke up with her over that, she was probably better off without him. No, he must have really loved her, having spent so much money in the first place. She was one lucky lady. She didn't deserve my pity. I needed that ring so much more than her. I was convinced of that. For the first time in my life, I was somebody. Well, still somebody without friends, while the rest of them got to hang out after work. Maybe I could save up a bit and join them for my twenty-fifth birthday. But that was ten months away. And I should really set something aside for a decent TV. One where the picture wouldn't cut out at crucial moments. Even if it was just another nineteen inch. Then having to stay at home wouldn't be so bad. Besides, I needed the TV for inspiration. Lean on other people to create my imaginary social life. Birthday parties, business soirees, dinner with Brett's parents. I chose my excuses carefully. No concerts, no movies. Nothing that could set me up for a false answer. I had already learned that in high school.

So tonight we had a late dinner at Brett's boss's house. And his wife was a gourmet chef. Chicken in a white wine sauce with miniature potatoes, which I had recently caught on *Rachael Ray*. On the way home Brett and I would stop for a coffee. But too far out of the way to catch up with the rest of the gang over at the Metropolis.

On my way to work the next day I rehearsed my story. I would throw in a couple of remarks about Brett's great personal relationship with the boss. Morgan would eat that up.

Then I saw the police cruisers parked in front of our store. Two big burly cops blocked the entrance. Morgan was gesticulating wildly to one of them, an older Italian guy who was patiently taking notes. The other girls hovered around the entrance, looking perturbed.

I made my way over to Jenny. "What happened?"

The Italian guy turned to me. "You work here, Miss?"

"She's our receptionist," Morgan answered for me.

The cop nodded briefly. "Alright, ladies, if you could all get into the cars and accompany us to the station, we need to take your statements. After that, you'll be free to go."

We'd had a break-in. The safe had been opened. The entire cash earnings for the week were gone. Two laptop computers, the in-house stereo, and the big screen TV from the lounge were also missing. And yet strangely enough, there was no sign of a forced entry. No smashed glass. Even the alarm system had been properly disabled. The robbers must not only have had a key, they somehow knew the code. This, of course, pointed to us employees.

"The girls were all together at a night club," Morgan said, still short of breath. "With the exception of Corinne here." She put a bony hand on my shoulder. "She had dinner with her fiancé."

The big Italian guy took note, then looked right at me. "Miss, if you could give us the name and address…"

"What?" I stared at him like a deer caught in the headlights.

"The name and address of your fiancé."

* * * *

Michael Palmer

About a week before we would be cleaning out our office, I actually caught a break, if you want to call it that. I had forwarded my resume to a small weekly paper called *The Benchmark*. It was aimed at the campus crowd. While they weren't currently hiring in their graphics department, they were actively looking for an advertising sales rep. After the interview, Karen agreed to meet me for lunch. She had suggested the *Mandarin Orange*, a small self-serve Chinese place near the MIT campus. It was crowded with students and college personnel. Not the kind of ambience I would normally go for. But the food was good and affordable, something we needed to consider given our financial situation. I was pretty low on cash. I even had to put the $9.16 lunch on my credit card. The guy behind me gave me the evil eye for holding up the line.

As I sat alone at one of the corner tables, I hoped Karen would show up soon. They had offered me the job. She would see that as good news. The base salary was a pittance, of course, but I was assured of endless earning potential on commission. A sheer marvel they had to post the job four times!

I'll admit I was a bit sore. I had long wanted to put out my own student paper. I had considered it years ago. But with our business cash strapped as it was, I simply didn't have the start-up capital. And now I got to work for someone else cashing in on my idea.

But Karen would see it as a step in the right direction. For now, I had a job. I was officially employed. She would never have supported me branching out into another business venture.

Where was Karen? She was supposed to meet me half an hour before. She was even less supportive than I thought. Perhaps she was already at her lawyer's. So maybe not a bluff after all. I checked my watch and gave her fifteen more minutes.

Why would Karen stand me up like that? Probably another emergency with her father. Would it never end? He had been sick the last couple of days with some virus that was making the rounds at the nursing home. According to Karen, he was "at death's door." Yeah, right. Just how many more times did we have to go through this? He had more lives than a cat.

I finally got up and left. What more did she want from me? I had even accepted that stupid job offer just to appease her. Apparently that still wasn't enough. I drove around aimlessly in an effort to cool off. The last thing we needed was another fight. I must have spent about an hour just circling around. When I finally tried to turn into our subdivision, the road was closed off. Police and ambulance cars were parked on both sides of the street. Yellow tape blew in the wind, like some movie prop. For a second I thought a crew was filming in our subdivision. I inched my way forward and rolled the window down.

"Sir," one of the cops, a young athletic guy with dark skin and a military buzz cut, yelled, "you can't go through here. Police investigation."

I diligently gave him my name and address. I was just trying to get home.

"Sorry, you're gonna have to pull over." He pointed to the curb.

I obliged and parked the car, and immediately got taken in for questioning.

"There has been an incident at your apartment building," an older, white-haired officer informed me on our way over to the station. "A forty-four-year-old female apparently fell off her balcony. A possible suicide, but we're still investigating."

What did that have to do with me? I didn't know half the people in our building. Plus, I had been away from the scene. I couldn't have seen or heard anything. Probably just routine.

"The victim has been identified by one of the neighbors as Karen Palmer. That's your wife, right?"

"What?" I felt all the blood drain from my body.

"I'm sorry," the officer said calmly. "I'm afraid your wife is dead."

* * * *

Trish Grady

"Trish, I'm telling you, he's cheating on you." My mother's voice sounded shrill on the other end. Just like my own when I got upset. "A guy doesn't just start working out without telling his wife. And those fitness places, they're pick-up spots!"

"Lots of people go there to work out," I replied.

"Single people, and married ones looking for a fling! Trish, hun, you better prepare yourself. Don't get hosed in the divorce! Bill's making a good salary. He owes you—" Mother was on a roll now, "—child and spousal support. You have a right to all that. Plus compensation for pain and suffering, emotional abuse…. You start collecting some hard evidence, and you build yourself a good, strong case. Let's see how much his mistress likes him penniless…"

His mistress. His fling. The other woman. No matter what you called her, she remained a faceless dark cloud hanging over my marriage. And it's not like I hadn't known all along. Of course, Bill would have brushed it off, claiming I watched too much TV. And I have to admit, there was something oddly comforting in seeing the rich and beautiful in that same predicament. Maybe that was what drew me to *Crystal Falls*. Jake cheated on Ivy. But Ivy had gotten her revenge—half of his fashion empire—and so would I.

On November 22 I rented a car. My mother was my only confidante. Talking to anybody else was pointless because they would just be on his side. With my mom taking over babysitting duties, I made my way to the car rental place that cold November night. I got myself a blue Honda Civic, one of those imports Bill hated so much.

I waited outside the bank, a good way off from the streetlight. He left on time. So where was he heading? The gym? Definitely not home. He turned north on Laramie Avenue, apparently headed for I-290. I followed him at a safe distance. Then I almost lost him when he merged onto I-294. I frantically searched through my purse for some change. Of all things, he had to pick a toll route! With all the car chases on TV, nobody ever takes a toll route.

He continued heading north, then west onto US-14. Where was he going? We didn't know anybody out here. Right, we didn't. But he obviously did.

He turned right onto, what I later learned from police records, was Rand Road. He was speeding now, and I had problems keeping up. I was angry and didn't care anymore whether he saw me. We were too far out for "clients." Mount Prospect had its own banks. He owed me an explanation. And it better be something good!

Suddenly he hit the brakes full force. The tires squealed, and I heard the sick crunch of metal hitting metal. He had struck something. I slammed my brakes and came to a screeching halt. Something like a bike wheel flew through the air, over my car, and into the darkness. For a moment Bill and I were both stopped in the middle of the road. Then, as I shakily opened my door to get out, I saw him take off. Behind me, two more cars came to a sudden stop.

"What happened?" someone yelled.

"I... I don't know. Someone just hit that cyclist."

I rushed to the ditch, frantically searching for the biker's body. What would I find? What if it was really just a body? I was not prepared for that. He had to be alive. "Oh please, let him be alive," I kept repeating under my breath.

The young man who had stopped his car behind me was the first to see him. "He's over there," he yelled. "Call an ambulance!"

"Call an ambulance," I shouted to a woman who might have been his passenger. Without hesitation she obliged.

I followed the young man into the ditch. The bike was there, all mangled up and barely recognizable. I made out a dark figure on the ground, barely recognizable as human.

"Is he alive?" I shrieked.

"I...I think so," the young man replied. "Wait...I can hear him breathing."

I rushed to his side and instinctively placed my hand on the biker's head.

The young guy grabbed my wrist. "Don't move him. We don't know what kind of injuries he's got. The ambulance will be here soon," he told the victim, who was still lying motionlessly on the ground. "They'll be here soon. Can you hear me?"

The figure groaned. He was alive. Alive!

"Is there anything we can do?" I asked, my voice trembling in the dark.

"Let's just keep him warm for now," the young guy said, taking off his jacket and carefully draping it over the biker's torso. Was he expecting me to give up my coat too? I was shivering as it was, and my teeth were chattering.

"They'll be here soon, buddy. Hang in there." He just kept repeating that over and over for what seemed like an eternity. "We're gonna stay with you. Just hang in there." The victim groaned back. At least he seemed to be able to hear us. That had to be a good sign, right? Oh, please, please, I silently begged, let that be a good thing.

"I...I can't feel my legs," he whispered suddenly, his voice barely audible.

"I can hear the ambulance," the young guy said. "They're here, they're here. You're gonna be alright, buddy, just hang in there."

Stephen Dowell

I stopped working weekends and went back to her store a couple more times, under the lamest of excuses. Mother still wasn't feeling up to it. If I could just borrow some brochures, I would certainly bring them back. Her name was Jillian, I found out. She had opened the shop after her best friend had been diagnosed with breast cancer.

"I was with Andrea through most of her chemotherapy treatments," Jillian told me. "But when we inquired with the hospital staff, nobody specifically catered to patients with medical hair loss. A few beauty salons offered a limited selection of wigs. But that's not the answer." She looked at me intently. I knew nothing about wigs or hair salons—wasn't that obvious?—but was touched she'd waste an explanation on me. "Just think about it. Who wants to try on a wig in front of all the other customers who go there with a full head of hair? It's uncomfortable, to say the least. I mean, just look at your mother. She doesn't even want to come here. And I have tried my best to be that safe haven for people with nowhere else to go."

"Right." She certainly was a safe haven for me. And I had no place else to go.

"About Mother, it's not looking good," I said. "The doctors aren't giving her much time." I felt a knot in my stomach. Jillian was a people person. Seeing through my lies wouldn't take her long. The time had come to write Mother's exit arc, as Irene would have called it.

"That must be hard for you." Jillian gently squeezed my arm. "How much time have they given her?"

"It could be a matter of days." And then that lie would, finally, be off the table.

She nodded sympathetically. "Listen," she said, "I'm about to close the shop for today and well, I normally don't do this with clients but, technically, you haven't bought anything yet, which makes you not really a client, I guess. Well then, how would you like to have dinner with me?"

I should have said no. That would have been the right thing to do. But guess what, I did the wrong thing. And before I knew it, we were going out.

* * * *

I only got to see Jillian on weekends due to our opposing schedules. I always drove out to New Haven. After all, I couldn't take her where people knew my late wife. Mother was still hanging in there, but getting worse by the minute.

"What's her name?" Jillian asked me over coffee one night. We were sitting outside on the patio of a cozy little Italian place, watching the people pass by.

"What?"

"What's your mother's name?" she wanted to know.

"Margaret." I should have pronounced her dead several weeks ago. I fumbled through my pockets and pulled out my cigarettes and lighter. Jillian shook her head.

"Look, I understand you're going through a tough time right now," she said slowly, "but it seems just…"

"What?" I asked innocently.

"Well, I don't know how to say it… but here's your mother, dealing with lung cancer, and you're still lighting up. How do you think she'd feel about that?"

I had quit drinking for Irene. Now smoking for Jillian? I reluctantly slipped the smokes back into my pocket.

"Here." She smiled and stretched out her open hand. "You give me those, and I'll dispose of them for you." I sighed and surrendered my last pack. I'd have to stop at a gas station on the way home.

"The lighter, too," she insisted. I rolled my eyes. A woman at the next table smiled. We probably sounded like an old married couple.

"Wow, look at that line now." Jillian pointed to the entrance. "Good thing we got here early."

At least fifteen parties must have been waiting to be seated, and among them—what on earth was she doing out here??!—my foreman, ehm, forewoman. Monstercheeks.

* * * *

37

Corinne Prichett

I don't think I was ever considered a real suspect in the burglary. A 5'3" girl just isn't likely to hoist a 90" flat screen out the front door. But my big fat lie about a fiancé was enough to disgrace me. The humiliation of twenty-four years in poverty came crashing down in a big public showdown. There was no fiancé, no big fancy dinners or business meetings. I was simply someone at the bottom of the social ladder. Morgan looked at me like a five-year-old who had just learned that Santa Claus, the Easter Bunny, and the Tooth Fairy didn't exist, all in one day. What a big fat liar I was! And—even more despicable—what kind of person would keep another woman's engagement ring? I'll tell you: the desperate kind.

While lying about your marital status isn't, technically, grounds for dismissal, I saw myself forced to quit. Back to minimum wage. After all, I couldn't go back to the employment agency that had, no doubt, gotten an earful about their applicant.

I found work in a candy factory, where I covered the early shift. Another job standing on my feet all day. Licorice and gummy bears at six in the morning. Endless conveyor belts and mind-numbing work like sorting out the deformed pieces, the happy faces that were less than perfectly round. You could eat off the belt, as much as you wanted. I think my supervisor expected me to, judging by the size of the apron he outfitted me with. It constantly got caught and posed a sizable work hazard.

I made no friends there, either. The older women didn't like me. I was probably one of them college kids, not cut out for hard work and surely gone in no time. They probably had a pool going behind my back.

After my shift I usually just walked straight home. I collapsed onto my rollaway bed and gave my sore feet a rest. Sometimes I tried to watch a little TV. But it got increasingly frustrating, with the picture cutting out more and more frequently. I was still saving up for a new one, though it seemed like a faraway dream now.

I had consigned most of my fancy work outfits at a small second-hand store. No need for me to dress up now. I missed it. I missed being someone. Within a week I had fallen from career woman to a minimum wage worker in a tent-like apron. A slob who ate off a belt. Disgusting.

I lay on my bed staring at my ceiling, too tired to make myself a tea, when someone rang my bell. I reluctantly got up.

"Who is it?" I yawned into the intercom. Probably the super. I sheepishly scanned the calendar. No, the rent wasn't due for eight more days.

"Corinne, is that you? It's me, Jenny."

Jenny? What was she doing here? As if I hadn't experienced enough humiliation, I'd now be forced to show her how I lived. Too late to avoid further embarrassment. She already knew I was home. Note to self: next time don't answer the intercom.

"Take the stairs," I cautioned through the speaker. "The elevator might get stuck again." I reluctantly buzzed her up.

"Hey," I forced a pained smile when she made it to my door. "Sorry, I wasn't expecting company."

"That's okay." She shook her head, sporting some brand-new blonde extensions. They looked good, though a bit wet. I was debating whether to say something, but it felt too awkward. This wasn't the right time to comment on her hair. But why had she come here? She unbuttoned her coat and kicked off her shoes, an unnecessary gesture in light of my grungy, old, loose parquet flooring. Keeping her shoes on was actually safer. That way she wouldn't risk splinters.

"Here, let me take that for you." I slowly hung up her coat, wondering what to say next. By now she knew I wasn't Miss High Society. But the prison cell look of my pad must still have come as a shock. How much furniture would a prison cell hold, anyway? It would probably, at the very least, have a chair beside that desk.

"Would you like some tea?" I asked. It was pretty much the only thing I could offer. Either that or water. Oh wait, I still had a sample of those fruit drink crystals.

"Tea would be nice," Jenny replied. "It's nasty outside." She ran her hands through her damp hair.

"Sorry about my place." I tried to sound casual as I slowly let the water flow into the kettle. "I know it looks…"

"Hey, it's a lot cleaner than my pad." She grinned. "Looks like a bomb went off there. Mostly my roommate's fault though, I swear."

I shrugged. "I don't have enough stuff to create a mess." It was really that simple. I was done pretending. "I'm poor. And there you have it."

"Listen," she said, "I'm sorry. I'm really sorry I didn't come out to see you sooner. It's just… the whole thing's been so stupid. So utterly stupid." Her voice was angry now. "Morgan acted like a complete moron, freaking out like that. I mean, it's none of her business whether you're engaged or not. Who cares? And did she really think you broke in and took her stupid TV?"

"I don't know." I sighed. "But you can see, here's my TV, and it's a total piece of crap." I kicked the screen with my foot, which sometimes momentarily brought back the picture. "Listen, I don't mean to be rude, but I really don't wanna talk about it anymore."

She pressed her lips together and slowly shook her head. "But I need to talk about it. I owe you an apology. A big, fat apology."

"It's okay," I dismissed. "Wasn't your fault. You really didn't need to come here. I'm alright and—"

"No," she said, cutting me off, "it's not that. Jazz did it. He took my keys and made copies. He said he had lost the one I gave him to my place. And stupid me, I believed him. I actually trusted the guy! And I really had no idea he knew that stupid code. He must have looked over my shoulder at some point. But I found one of the laptops in his trunk and then I knew… Oh, Corinne, I am so sorry."

I just stood there, not knowing what to say. Jazz did it. He had wrecked my life.

"I'm so sorry," Jenny repeated. "Can you forgive me?"

"Of course." I sighed. "It's not your fault, anyway. I made up that whole lie, and I ended up paying for it. I certainly learned my lesson. I looked like a complete idiot."

She sank down onto my rollaway bed and stared up at the ceiling. Just like I had a few moments ago. But I no longer cared if she noticed the water damage, two deep, dark, circular clouds looming dangerously over my bed. Maybe it was time to move it again. In a dump like this, a bed on wheels came in handy.

"You know, I quit," Jenny said now slowly.

"What?"

"You were right. They really were a bunch of phonies."

"I never said that," I objected. "If anything, I was the phony!"

"No." She shook her head. "In a way, you showed 'em all up. Clothes, money, status, it's all crap. And if that's all they're after, then I don't wanna be there either."

"Can you afford that?" I looked at her skeptically.

"No," she laughed. "But I'd rather be poor with you. And by the way, I have a spare TV, if you want it. The picture's a bit yellow, but at least it's got picture. Man, that black screen is annoying."

I walked over and turned it off.

"Hey, leave it on," she protested. "*Crystal Falls* is coming up!"

* * * *

Michael Palmer

"Was your wife depressed? In any state of distress lately?" Detective Doyle, the older, white-haired officer who had driven me to the station, asked me.

"No, not that I can think of," I answered tonelessly. Angry and frustrated, yes. But not depressed. That just wasn't Karen.

"Nothing unusual in the recent past? Nothing that might have upset her?"

"Her dad has been sick for years. That's been hard on her. On all of us. He's got Alzheimers. We had to put him in a care facility a couple of weeks ago. Karen didn't feel good about that. But it... that wouldn't have made her jump off the building..." I could barely bring myself to say those last words. Karen was dead. I couldn't wrap my mind around that. My whole body felt numb, heavy, lifeless. Mere breathing seemed like an enormous, useless effort.

Detective Doyle came right to the point. "How would you describe the state of your marriage?"

I swallowed. I knew he was going to ask that. But would she rather have jumped off a building than stay married to me?

"We've been going through a rough time. I'm not gonna lie to you. I had to close down my business. And then the strain of my father-in-law living with us for the past three years... We had to take care of him constantly. It was hard. It took a toll on us. On our marriage. But things were just starting to turn around." I cleared my throat, but the lump remained. "I had an interview today. I got a new job with a paper. Karen was supposed to meet me for lunch..."

Detective Doyle nodded. "Where were you between one and three this afternoon?"

I looked at him in shock and disbelief, cold chills running down my spine and my palms turning sweaty. He could not possibly think...

"Routine question," he simply said. "I have to ask you, Mr. Palmer: where were you between one and three this afternoon?"

"I... I finished my job interview around... twelve thirty, I guess. Then I went over to the restaurant where Karen was supposed to meet me. The place is called the *Mandarin Orange*. It's near the

MIT campus. I had lunch there and waited for Karen 'til almost two, I think."

Detective Doyle took note, intermittently looking up from his paper. "And when your wife didn't show, did you make any attempt to get a hold of her?"

I shook my head. I hadn't bothered to check on her. I knew it must have looked awful. I was kicking myself. Why hadn't I checked on her? 'Cause I never suspected anything to be wrong. I thought she had simply stood me up. Karen had a temper. It wouldn't have been the first time.

"I didn't have my cell phone on me. And I was short of change," I muttered, realizing how lame that sounded. "I just waited and then finally got up and left. I was angry that Karen hadn't shown up. So I drove around for a while, trying to cool off. I didn't want another fight."

Detective Doyle looked at me, and I was wondering what he saw. A guy who had just killed his wife?

"Do you have a place to stay for a while?" he asked now. "Until we're finished with the investigation, we can't let you return to your apartment."

I nodded slowly. I'd have to call Julian. I'd have to tell him his sister was dead.

* * * *

He came to pick me up at the station. I was relieved to see a familiar face in this nightmare. Like he had simply come here to wake me up. But Julian himself looked tired, his dark hair falling over his eyes as he slowly made his way down the corridor. His shoulders slouched, his jacket was sloppily done up, he had missed most of the buttons. He kept shuffling his feet, and his dirty sneakers made tiny, rhythmic squeaking sounds across the linoleum. From far enough away, he looked like a college kid. But up close, I saw a man as broken as me. I realized that right at that moment he was the only person in the world who understood how I felt.

"Michael." He hugged me tight. "I'm so... so sorry." His voice broke.

Officer Doyle discreetly left the room.

"How did this happen?" Julian looked at me, and I could see the agony in his eyes. "This is all my fault. I shouldn't have moved Dad. I was just trying to help... I didn't know she'd take it this hard..."

"It's not your fault," I interrupted him sternly.

"I'm so sorry, Karen," he whispered. "So sorry."

"Julian, don't do this to yourself. This is not your fault, do you hear me?" I grabbed him by the shoulder and looked him in the eye. "Listen to me. This is nobody's fault, okay?"

* * * *

We spent the next few days at Julian's place in a daze. We drank too much, barely ate, and couldn't sleep. I felt like I had been hit by a truck, and I was concerned about Julian. He was Karen's little brother. She had always been protective of him. Not sure if she would have cared about me at this point, but she would have hated seeing Julian like that. He was always the optimist, the kind of guy life couldn't knock down. Even when our business went under, he never took it as hard as me. We had experience, he had insisted. That was something no one could take away from us. We would land other jobs. Julian, always reminding me things would work out. And now he spent the days pacing across the kitchen floor, waiting for some news from the police.

"Why haven't they called yet?" He poured himself another whiskey, missing the glass and spilling most of the contents on the kitchen counter. "Don't you think they should have some autopsy results by now?"

"It can't be long," I said tiredly. I had no idea how much time an autopsy would take. But what difference did it make? What more was there to say? When you plunge from the eleventh floor, the cause of death is no big mystery. What caused her to plunge from the eleventh floor, however, was one big mystery to me. Yes, we had problems. But Karen simply wasn't the type to end her own life. She was a fighter, tough as nails. It's what attracted me to her in the first place. And it's what ended up driving a wedge between us. I was a failure in her eyes. But she cared deeply about her dad, if not about me anymore. She would never have left him behind. Her death didn't make any sense.

44

"I can't sit here anymore." Julian reached for his car keys behind the kitchen counter. "I'm gonna go to the office. Clean out the rest of our stuff. I might as well do something."

"I'll come with you." I reached for my coat. I had to; Julian was in no shape to drive.

"You don't have to come," he offered. "Just stay here, try to get some rest."

"No." I shook my head. "I'll clean out the office with you. Let's finish this together."

* * * *

We're always taught that life has good and bad days. I now know that some days are so phenomenally bad, they seem unreal later. Looking back you think I couldn't possibly have gone through all that and still be here. The day of my arrest was certainly like that. There I was with Julian, packing up our things. Little was said; this was a day of total defeat. Ten years gone down the drain. And yet, my business didn't matter anymore. Karen was gone, and the tragedy of her death was all just too much. At some point I simply turned numb. Maybe that was my body's protective mechanism kicking in. A natural defense system against too much pain.

The police cruiser pulled up in front of our office. Finally some news. Maybe it would bring Julian some peace.

Officer Doyle stepped in through the door slowly. "Mr. Palmer, you're under arrest. You have the right to remain silent. Anything you say can and will be used against you in a court of law..."

To this day the scene seems like out of a bad movie: Julian's horrified expression—there had to be some mistake—the empty office space spinning around me, the officers guiding me to the car. Total strangers stared at me in the street, inevitably jumping to their own false conclusions. And I kept wanting to object. But like a bad dream, I couldn't get a word out. I didn't do it, didn't do it, didn't do it. It just kept pounding through my head. I would have thrown myself off that balcony before I would have pushed her.

* * * *

I slowly learned the details through my lawyer, Mr. Joe Percara. He was a tall, skinny man with receding dark hair and a beak-like nose. To this day I don't know what to make of him. He stared at me like a vulture hovering over a wounded animal, and devoured the smallest detail I threw him. What bothered me most was that I couldn't tell whether he believed me. I thought it vital—essential— that he, my lawyer, believed in my innocence. How else was he going to stand up for me in court? I didn't want someone to defend me out of obligation. I needed his conviction. But he never gave me that satisfaction.

The coroner had ruled out suicide. Karen had fallen backwards over the balcony and, in a frantic effort to save herself, had ripped off part of the wind chimes. The very wind chimes I had hated so much. The chimes I used to tape together. The ones she would untie just to bug me. Now they would haunt me forever.

The police had found a small step ladder on the balcony, along with some plants Karen had partly repotted. Percara was going for "accidental death," the only other option. But our financial troubles were evident. The life insurance policy gave me a motive. And my alibi was less than stellar. From twelve thirty on—the time I had left my job interview—until three, I could not prove my whereabouts. The *Mandarin Orange* was busy that day. I couldn't remember seeing a single familiar face. The check-out girl, who barely spoke any English, conceded she might have seen me before. But she couldn't remember a time or day. And the hour I had spent driving around only made matters worse.

Percara took an awkward seat beside me, his long limbs dangling beside the chair. There remained something birdlike about him, and I was concerned what he would project to the jurors.

"Joe, we've been over this," I said tiredly. "A million times."

He stared at me from the side. A long, hard stare, laced with contempt. "I'm not gonna lie to you, Michael. Things aren't looking good. We need someone to back up your story. Someone who saw you at that restaurant."

"I told you a million times I didn't know anybody there. It was lunchtime. It was really crowded. Some guy behind me got mad 'cause I didn't have enough cash on me and had to pay by Visa. I was holding up the line and…"

"And you're telling me this now?" Percara asked incredulously.

"I didn't know the guy. I can't even remember what he looked like," I replied unhelpfully.

"Not that," Percara waived off impatiently. "You paid by Visa?"

* * * *

Trish Grady

Someone brought me a blanket—I didn't even know they had those at a police station. But I guess it makes sense, what with officers taking naps between shifts. I was freezing cold and in shock. My whole body just kept shaking. I asked if I could have some tea. But I spilled most of that with my trembling hands.

"Will he be alright?" I asked through chattering teeth. The victim, I had learned, was nineteen-year-old Christopher Berndt. He had talked to us. That had to mean he'd be alright, right? Nonsense; on TV people always took a turn for the worse. One minute they would give out vital information, you know, who dunnit. And before the next commercial break they were gone.

"We don't know yet," the young policewoman opposite the desk said quietly. "It's too early to say. But you were the first at the scene. Can you tell us what you saw?"

"It was dark… he was speeding… I heard a crash and then this tire flew through the air. I instinctively ducked and…" I burst into tears. I cried and cried, sobbed uncontrollably. I could feel my make-up running down my cheeks. Good thing I wasn't there for a mug shot. All those awful pictures you see of celebrities in the paper, and then you wonder, "Is that really her?" I was certain that, at that point, I was unrecognizable. Then again, I wasn't famous. Nobody cared what I looked like. Nobody cared about me, period.

"Mrs. Grady," the officer said in an oddly soothing voice, "can you describe the vehicle for me?"

Describe the vehicle? I slowly looked up, strangely comforted that she had addressed me by my name. She remembered my name.

"I can give you his name and the license plate," I heard myself say. And then I did. There, I had turned him in. It was the most important decision I had to make in my entire life, and it only took me a split second. It was more of an automatic response, the kind you exhibit during a fire drill. I turned him in. I tried to remain calm and proceed to the nearest exit. I wasn't aware of the collateral damage back then. You just get out of the burning building. You don't count the cost.

* * * *

A week later, my daughter still refused to talk to me. And the heartbreak of having to explain his father's imprisonment to my eight-year-old son was beyond words.

"Is Dad sorry he hit that man?" he whispered when I tucked him in that night.

"Yes, he is." I kissed his forehead. "Yes he is. We're all very sorry."

But while I was sure that Bill, indeed, was sorry for the accident, I couldn't help but wonder. Was he sorry the victim—a nineteen-year-old kid—was now a quadriplegic, confined to a bed when he should be playing sports with his friends? Or was Bill just sorry he got caught? Sorry he had cheated on me? No, probably not the last one. But I don't want anyone to think revenge motivated me. Standing there in the ditch that night with the mangled bike and the helpless, dark figure hovering between life and death made me realize one thing. I would have turned in anybody—my mother, even myself. Yes, I would have turned myself in. But Bill... he took off, he left a kid to die. How could I ever have trusted him to care for me?

49

Stephen Dowell

"Stephen, stop dragging me," Jillian complained, still out of breath. "Who or what exactly are we running from?"

"Monstercheeks," I replied, pulling her into the nearest store entrance.

"What?"

"My foreman, ehm, forewoman. Monstercheeks. I told her I needed some time off... for mother, you know. I can't let her see me here."

Jillian looked at me hurt. "You used your mother as an excuse? And what's that, calling her Monstercheeks? That is horribly, horribly insulting!"

"Hey, I didn't come up with that name," I said in my defense. "Everybody calls her that."

She threw her arms up. "And if everybody jumps off a bridge?"

I rolled my eyes. I hadn't heard that one since I was ten.

"Quick," she said, "three positive things."

"What?"

"My grandma used to say, even if you don't like someone, you can always say three positive things about them. About everyone. So, give me three positive things."

About Monstercheeks? I thought hard. How was I supposed to... "She's an excellent forklift driver," I said. "It's true, she really is. I mean, maneuvering around these narrow aisles is hard. And you've gotta lift these heavy pallets, hundreds of pounds, especially when you're dealing with sand. And all the time you're working overhead. You gotta lift them as much as three, four stories high. It's dangerous work and—"

"Stephen!" She threw her arms up in the air. "Enough about the forklift! Tell me something positive about her."

"I don't really know her. It's not like we're dating or something."

She quietly shook her head. She was disappointed in me, I could tell.

"Look, I'm sorry," I said. It was the best I could offer.

"No, you don't understand. That's what I deal with every day. Women feeling awful because they've lost all their hair. They're afraid to go out because people will stare and see how bad they look. I thought you of all people would understand, with your mother going through something like that. And then you go and make such a horrible, insensitive remark…"

"I'm sorry," I repeated. "I am truly, truly sorry." And I was. Though I doubted Monstercheeks cared what she looked like. She really only cared we unloaded the trucks. Jillian reached for my hand. Did that mean I was forgiven? We silently walked on.

"One more thing," she finally said after an uncomfortable silence. "Why did you lie to her? I mean, I don't get it. What's wrong with only doing five shifts a week? You have a right to have the weekends off. And she's not working either! So why lie about it? And drag your mother into it?"

"It's not that easy," I replied tiredly. "We're really short-staffed."

"But honesty is important. It's important to me. I've been through enough bad relationships. I want an honest guy." She looked me straight in the eyes. "You wouldn't lie to me, would you?"

* * * *

Jeremy Lawren

I was against it from the start. But Rob was adamant. We needed something new. After three years, an oil baron, a fashion empire, and two feuding drug lords simply weren't cutting it. This time, we'd go for some real drama.

I made one last ditch effort to talk Rob out of it. But to no avail. He would go through with the contest.

"There's really nothing in here, Rob," I said, pointing to the basket full of mail. Of course there wasn't. After all, people who wasted their time watching *Crystal Falls* really couldn't have much else going on. "There's nothing here our writers can't fabricate in a bigger, better version."

"That's beside the point." Rob emphatically shook his head. "Listen, Jerry. Take my word for it, you got a lot to learn about showbiz, kid. It doesn't matter if you think it's a good story. It's a true story. You can't buy that kind of credibility. People dig that. That contest was brilliant, I'm telling you. We made all the papers. All the important ones, anyway. When was the last time our show got that much publicity? Ratings are up, and we haven't even started! Now," he grabbed a fistful of entries and twirled them through the air, "you get back on it and find me ten tearjerkers in there."

In moments like that I really hated him. And myself for needing him. Well, maybe I didn't. I'd work on my resume again. Writing the gardening section in a local town cryer seemed like a step up from this. That's all I ever wanted to do, anyway. Write. Not necessarily in the gardening section. Little did I know my first writing gig would be a log for the police.

* * * *

Corinne Prichett

I'm not sure what you want to hear from me, I don't know anything about Rob's death. But if it helps you in your investigation, I will recount the events from the time I got here.

It started with the notice I was one of the finalists. It seemed too good to be true. I had never won anything in my life! Could it be a scam? I reread the letter, but it seemed authentic. Yes, it came from the address I had mailed my entry to. And no, no hidden fees or charges. All expenses paid… They really weren't after my money. Just after my story. Wow. I had to sit down. And while I understood I hadn't won yet, I was one of the finalists, nonetheless. A free trip to LA—nobody could take that from me! And a good shot at winning the two hundred grand. I phoned my friend Jenny 'cause I just had to tell someone.

* * * *

Stephen Dowell

Crap. I thought once I had mailed in that entry I would never have to write anything again. And now this. You want to know what happened?

I was drunk when I found out I was a winner. There, happy now? I said it, I was drunk. I'd been to see Jillian. She was about to close up shop for the day. If only I had waited, let's say ten, fifteen minutes, everything would've been fine. But I really wanted to see her, right? So I get there just as she walks out with Mrs. Wellish, one of my former neighbors. She'd accompanied her sister to have a wig fitted. Like she was rubbing it in. She'd accompanied her sister, while I... naw, she couldn't have known I never went with Irene. Anyway, how was I holding up, she wanted to know. Irene was such a lovely lady. They sure missed her down by the travel center. She'd been by far the most helpful of all their staff. It surely must be hard for me. You have no idea, I thought angrily. Just SHUT UP! I could feel Jillian stare at me the whole time. She just looked at me, and I could tell what must have been going through her head. As soon as Mrs. Wellish got into her car, Jillian walked back inside. She slammed the door right in my face. She never said a word.

I knew right then I had lost her. There was nothing I could do. I stayed out most of the night drinking 'cause I couldn't bear the thought of going home. I slept in my truck, and eventually made it back to my place sometime in the early morning hours. And there was the letter. You've been chosen... At that moment I didn't feel chosen for anything. I would have gladly put a gun to my head, but had the distinct feeling that would disappoint Irene somehow.

* * * *

Michael Palmer

I appreciate the opportunity to give my side of the story, even if some of it might not be pretty. But you want to hear the truth, right? Well, the truth isn't always pretty.

You've been chosen… Yeah, just like one of those credit card offers. You've been preapproved, aren't you lucky?

I'll admit I was in a foul mood the day I got the notice. Percara and I were engaged in an ongoing battle about some of his legal fees. He had merely achieved a dismissal for me. A good lawyer would have restored my reputation with a "not guilty" verdict. Then the fees would have been justified. Now he was just the guy "who got me off." It bothered me immensely. "Getting me off" implied I had somehow dodged my rightful sentence. It didn't proclaim my innocence. Clearly nobody believed me. Not even my own lawyer.

Alone at my breakfast table I kept staring at the letter. Would this finally be my chance? The longer I sat there, the more agitated I felt. I would have to think this through carefully. Very carefully. After all, I wouldn't want to make another spectacle of myself. I just wanted to set the record straight. But did I really want to go through with this? I finally realized I did when talking it over with Julian.

"I know it's tempting," he cautioned, "but ask yourself, is it really worth it? I mean, the case was dropped. That's the best you could ask for."

"No, a not guilty verdict would have been the best. And that's what I'm asking for. I want my life back. I want people to know I'm innocent."

"I know you're innocent," he assured me. "Your family is completely behind you. All I'm saying is I think you should just let the press die down. Try to rebuild your life."

But I would never be able to do that until people believed I was innocent in my wife's death. Yes, I would do the show. Even against my best friend's advice.

* * * *

55

Trish Grady

Let me start by saying I'm a huge fan of *Crystal Falls*, and Rob de Heer was one of the most charming and influential men I ever had the pleasure of meeting. I cannot begin to think who would want him dead! I would also like to mention that I am extremely grateful for the opportunity we were given here, and have nothing but good things to say about the way we, the contestants, were treated. And while some of the others seemed ungrateful from the start, I will certainly not take any of this for granted.

Yes, I remember the day I found out I was invited to come to LA. It was a happy moment, followed by severe disappointment. My daughter Megan threw a fit. Hadn't I done enough? I had already ruined everybody's lives. And now I had to embarrass her on national TV?

We could use the money, I tried to argue through her closed bedroom door. And I wouldn't actually be on TV. They would choose an actress for the part. Besides, none of her friends watched that show, anyway. She always said so herself. Still, she refused to come out. My mother finally told me to keep my voice down as the walls were paper thin. No need to get the whole neighborhood involved. I gave up. Why was I even bothering? If I wanted to do this, it was up to me. I had a right to live my own life, whether my selfish thirteen-year-old understood that or not. It should have been a happy—no, thrilling—moment. I wouldn't let her spoil it for me. Then I reread the letter and realized I was only one of the finalists. Maybe assuming I had already won was a bit hasty. But the trip was mine. And I'd get the chance to hang out at the *Crystal Falls* set! Besides, there couldn't be that many finalists. Whoever else would show up, they couldn't have possibly gone through an ordeal like mine.

* * * *

Jeremy Lawren

I wasn't there the afternoon the final four contestants arrived here in LA. Rob had sent me over to the post-production house, trying to establish cue sheets. We were using stock music in several scenes. The music needed to be logged for royalties, but hadn't been. You'd think after three seasons people would get the hang of it.

Rob introduced me to our finalists at dinner that night, over at the mansion. On this occasion he brought up shooting some behind-the-scenes footage to compile a little promo piece. Additional publicity, as he was quick to point out. And I suspect it was also part of the conditions for using the mansion, which usually came as a high-priced rental. But initially the reality shoot was not part of the plan. However, it later provided a valid excuse for me to move among the suspects.

I didn't like any of them, but had enough sense to realize I wasn't being objective. After all, they had cost me two months' worth of work. And how could we prove their stories weren't fiction, anyway?

Rob, of course, didn't care. "If we can't prove it, neither will anybody else!"

I shook hands with each one of the finalists and introduced myself as Jeremy. I hate being called Jerry. But it's what everyone on the set does.

I'm not sure what I was expecting. But nonsense like this inevitably draws the same lineup: the publicity hound, the gold digger, the next reality show star. At first glance, only Trish would have fit that description. A heavy-set blonde with a lifeless perm and unflatteringly tight jeans. That eager I-deserve-to-win gleam in her eyes, as alarming as her traffic-sign-red nail polish. She would have been better off competing for a complete make-over.

The other female, Corinne, was the complete opposite. While Trish talked at a million miles a minute, Corinne seemed quiet and withdrawn. Either too shy or too arrogant. She was pretty, with dark brown, shoulder-length hair and piercing blue eyes. A little too skinny for my liking. And let's not forget, this is California. I could throw a rock and hit someone good-looking. Yet, there was something different, almost regal, about her. And we were supposed to believe she had been poor all her life?

Michael could have passed as a regular on *Crystal Falls*. Tall, dark, and handsome—put him in a suit, and he could have been one of the lawyers. (Ironically, the guy had spent enough time around lawyers the last couple of years!) I would never have taken him as a business failure. He just looked like the picture of success. And maybe that's why I quickly found myself biased against him. He seemed to be working overtime trying to appear upright. Each sentence sounded carefully rehearsed. A PowerPoint of political correctness. A sharp contrast to Trish's bubbly ramblings and Corinne's reserve. I looked at Michael and inevitably found myself picturing him on the witness stand (and maybe that's where he still saw himself). His appearance must have swayed the jury. I was determined he wouldn't fool me. But would it work on Rob? Did he believe Michael was innocent? Actually, Rob wouldn't care. Just as long as we got a good story for our show.

And that's where I saw the problem with Stephen, our fourth contestant. There was no way to incorporate him into a soap. Not unless we happened to be shooting an episode in an Irish pub. He was actually Scottish, not Irish. Not that it mattered. He still wouldn't fit—even though our largely female audience would probably approve of him. His hands were rough, and his lips chapped, kinda like I would have expected from someone working in construction. His tousled, dirty blonde hair gave him a boyish air below the tough-guy surface. He mainly stuck to single-word answers and obviously knew nothing about our show. At times he was apologetic. But not to the point of being sincere. I wondered why he'd come. He seemed uncomfortable in this pompous villa. I almost had to laugh picturing this guy in a wig shop. He played with his dinner utensils and took a sip of water after almost every bite. I later learned he was attempting to kick a twenty-year smoking habit. Incidentally, he was also the only one to pass on the champagne.

"Tomorrow," Rob declared swankily, "Jerry will take you on a grand tour of the set. You get to meet the cast and crew. The whole nine yards. You get an exclusive behind-the-scenes look at the shoot. How is that for an experience?"

Trish's eyes lit up. Michael nodded politely. Corinne continued cutting her filet mignon, and Stephen, very obviously, didn't care.

* * * *

"And here's where we shoot some of the outdoor footage." I listlessly motioned to the small, pretty courtyard sporting a kidney-shaped swimming pool.

"So this is where Jack and Ivy are sipping their Margueritas," Trish said knowingly.

"You got it." I couldn't tell what annoyed me more, Trish's over-the-top adoration for this nonsense little show or the others' complete lack of appreciation. I could think of better ways to spend my afternoon, too. These guys at least had a shot at the money.

"So, how long before the producers make a decision?" Michael wanted to know.

"Sorry?" I asked, pretending not to follow.

"When are they gonna tell us who won?" Trish obviously felt the need to simplify.

I could feel all eyes on me now. "Well, Rob's still going over your entries. He just has to verify a few things," I said evasively. Not that I was really expecting him to. I was simply stalling. I had no idea if and when the producers would pick a winner. But I didn't feel like letting on about how low on the totem pole I really was.

"Does he think we made up our stories?" Trish sounded a bit shrill now, and a tad too defensive.

"No, no, certainly not." I quickly waved off. "Checking the entries is standard. Our legal department would be all over us if we didn't." I was kicking myself. Of all the submissions, why did I have to pick them? Well, I hadn't. Rob had singled them out as the most promising storylines for our show, in a desperate attempt to boost our ratings. But, hey, without me they would never have gotten this far! I was dreading entertaining this group for another two weeks. But then things changed unexpectedly.

The police later asked me if I had seen anything suspicious or noticed any changes in behavior or routines. As far as the contestants were concerned, I honestly couldn't tell. I'd known none of them long enough to determine what was usual for them. The only obvious change I noticed was in Rob himself.

Up to this point, he had shown no real interest in the contestants. They were mere mules pulling his publicity wagon. And judging by how quickly he had unloaded them on me, I braced myself for being at their beck and call for the next couple of weeks. I was positively stunned when I found Rob that night, late in his office, studying their initial entries.

"What are you doing?" I asked, leaning over his desk.

"They're certainly an interesting lot, those guys. Don't you think?"

"Hmm," I said half-heartedly. Not sure if I found them that extraordinary. Probably more ungrateful than I would have expected them to be. For two hundred grand you could fake a bit more enthusiasm. Maybe not the most motivated bunch.

"How did it go today?" Rob wanted to know.

"So-so. To be honest, with the exception of Trish, I don't think any of them are big fans of *Crystal Falls*. I think the only real draw is the money."

Rob laughed. "Ah, they may not admit to watching it. But we're on people's guilty pleasure list. You really think a guy like Stephen would admit to his construction buddies he's been watching *Crystal Falls*? Nah."

I was convinced that Stephen, indeed, had never watched. And Corinne was obviously only here for the cash. Michael? He had probably caught an episode here and there. But most likely just in the name of "research" for the contest. He was too professional to show up unprepared.

I'll admit I was a tad jealous. To make two hundred grand, I'd have to work for quite a while. I didn't even wanna do the math. It was too depressing.

I was, therefore, understandably pleased when Rob relieved me of my tour-guiding duties the next day.

"Let me spend some time with them," Rob said. "Maybe even with each of them separately. I wanna find out what makes them tick. Maybe we're on to something here. This could yield some pretty good material."

At the time I assumed he was talking about the spin-off reality shoot. Frankly, I didn't care. But as to whether there was anything out of the ordinary—yes. Rob's sudden personal interest in our contestants seemed highly unusual.

* * * *

His new plan to single them out was met with mixed emotions. While Trish relished the sudden attention given to her and her storyline—did this mean she was the front-runner?—Corinne seemed very uncomfortable. Hey, if I were a woman, I would've been too! She was obviously trying to avoid being alone with Rob. But at the same time you could tell she was torn. She still needed the money. Don't get me wrong, I'm not saying he was coming on to her. But I could see how she could take it that way. I mean, this was Rob. Rob, who had spent the better part of his life in this industry of sleazy compliments and obnoxious smiles. He simply didn't know how to work his way around "ordinary" people. Particularly those who weren't adoring fans of everything he'd ever done. He hit rock bottom with Stephen. Here the roles were strangely reversed. Rob would return, after time spent alone with him, alienated and confused.

"I just can't pin the guy down," he'd say, the frustration evident in his voice. "I just don't think he likes me."

More than half the people on the set don't, I added silently. And include me in that figure.

Michael, ever the professional, was more accommodating. He was certainly willing to give additional background information. Yet all the while he remained cautious, impenetrable, and painstakingly correct. He had clearly spent the past two years talking only through his lawyer. While Rob, on the other hand, was after the raw, straight goods. But why was he all of a sudden so bent on finding the truth behind each story? And what made him think he was getting it? How do you get the truth from a potential murderer, two liars, and someone yearning for their fifteen minutes?

* * * *

61

Rob's strange obsession with our contestants continued. Day after day, with everyone long gone, I would find him in his office. I don't know how many times he must have read over their submissions.

"We shot a bit of footage over at the mansion today," I informed him. "Just the contestants introducing themselves and talking about the show."

"Good." Rob nodded briefly. "I'll have a look through those tapes later. Just make sure you keep them all logged."

"I still don't see why you're so into the whole thing," I said truthfully. "I mean, the contest, alright. I see where you're going with this. It's new, it's publicity. And yes, ratings are up already. Congratulations. But as far as the contestants… you can keep going over their stories. I just don't think there's any more to it than what we already know."

"Maybe, maybe not," he replied mysteriously. "But let's just think here for a minute. Take someone like Trish, for example. The husband cheats on her. She's on to him. He causes a major accident and flees the scene. Now she turns him in. The jilted wife, vengeful, some may say. An honest, honorable citizen, say the others. She did this at her own expense. The husband's in jail. Now where's the child and spousal support coming from? But she did the right thing. She told the truth. Or did she?"

"I'm not sure where you're going with this," I replied.

"Work with me, Jerry. The husband's speeding along. He's driving way too fast, there's no question about that. But why was he speeding? Was it not because he was being followed?"

The thought had crossed my mind. I nodded slowly. "But she was never charged with anything," I pointed out.

"Right." Rob smiled. "But that's just one of them. Then there's Corinne. I mean, how can you be broke and that standoffish at the same time? It's like she doesn't even want our help. Or Stephen, constantly fidgeting around. The guy can't wait to get outta here. Wonder what he's been holding out on us. And Michael, well, who knows if he killed his wife? But did you know his father-in-law died shortly after? And let's not forget, Michael had just gotten a new job. Looks to me like someone was busy setting up a brand-new life."

"Or maybe you've just been watching too much TV," I said with a smirk.

"Ah, but the truth is stranger than fiction," he replied dramatically. The truth is stranger than fiction. It kept running through my mind when, a week later, Rob was found dead.

* * * *

I was the last to see him alive. Well, technically, the murderer was, I guess. But no matter how hard I tried to think about it, nothing about that night stood out for me. I had spent the entire afternoon on the set. I was tired and just wanted to get home. If only I could have gone straight to bed. But it was Friday—bar fight—night. So I'd have to make my usual stop at the police station and pick up my buddy Frank.

"Jerry, come here for a sec," Rob called after me when he saw me heading out. "How's our little shoot coming?"

The very question I was trying to dodge. It wasn't coming at all. We hadn't filmed any more footage over at the mansion. And I was sure he knew. Even a reality shoot needs some kind of action. But there was no plot. I held the camera while someone poured coffee or brushed his teeth. Not to mention the shameless plug for the mansion: the pool, the gym, the fancy counter tops. This was worse than a home movie. A colossal waste of time. Precisely why Rob didn't bother with it himself.

"I told you, we didn't get much past the introduction. It's not that easy. Give it a few days. They're not professional actors, you know." I glanced over his shoulder, feigning an interest in whatever he was doing. "You still going over the entries? Found anything new?"

"Maybe I have," Rob replied, a smug grin on his face. I wasn't the least bit curious.

"Just give me a couple more days," he said now, trying to sound mysterious. "I'm working on a real bombshell here."

I was used to Rob putting his publicity spin on things. Someone had to sell our show, right? But I did not believe for one second that he had actually found anything. And yet, I later dutifully reported it to the police. They searched Rob's files and found nothing.

"Listen, I gotta go. Remember Frank, one of our old camera guys? I need to bail him out again."

* * * *

By six thirty in the morning Frank and I were finally ready to leave the police station. I was tired. My head was pounding. Another bar fight, anger management, community service. Just how many more times did we have to go through this? And how much longer did I owe him for getting me this crappy gopher job on this stinking soap?

"Jeremy Lawren?" someone called after me. "You need to stay here."

I turned and saw one of the younger cops, about my age, with red hair and an ugly sunburn. What on earth could he want from me? I wasn't involved in the fight. I never was. I just came by here every other week to pick up Frank. Maybe some unpaid parking tickets? But Rob was supposed to cover those. After all, my job was to drive around for him. Wherever he wanted, whenever he wanted. Because I obviously didn't have a life.

I listlessly followed the young cop into his office. The sign on his desk spelled out his name as Detective J. V. Hail. An inappropriate name for someone who had so clearly been exposed to too much sun.

He motioned for me to sit down. "You work for Rob de Heer?"

I nodded. Oh please, not another person wanting a walk-on part. He would, no doubt, show up in the credits as *guy with sunburn*.

"Rob was found dead this morning," he said matter-of-factly.

I stared at him, unable to say anything. How do you adequately react to something like that?

"But... but I just talked to him last night," I finally stammered. "Do I need a lawyer?"

I'm not sure why I asked that particular question. It just seemed logical, I guess. Anything you say can and will be used against you in a court of law.

Detective Hail shook his head. "You certainly have the right to a lawyer. But I don't see why you would need one at this point. You were here last night. We can vouch for that. But now I'm curious. Why would you consider yourself a suspect?" He raised an eyebrow, obviously intrigued by my unsubstantiated request for a lawyer. "Would you say you had a motive for killing Rob?"

"No... no, of course not," I stammered. "I just thought... Well, why else would you call me into your office?"

He shrugged. "At this point I just need to ask you a few routine questions. You said you talked to Rob last night?"

"Yeah, I talked to him on my way out. He was still in his office over at Skyview. That was just around midnight. And then I came straight here. Where did you find him?" I should have asked earlier. Rob was dead, and I didn't have a single question about that? No wonder I looked suspicious. "Can you tell me what happened?" I added, hoping that would somehow make up for my gross display of disinterest.

"One of the cleaners at Skyview found him this morning," Detective Hail informed me. "He appears to have been stabbed."

"Do you have any suspects?" I asked.

He shook his head. "So far we don't have much to go on. But we are still in the early stages of the investigation. The autopsy on Rob's body will be later this afternoon. And of course we have to interview everyone involved with the production. You were his assistant; can you tell me anything? Any enemies he might have had?"

At this point I almost laughed out loud. That, of course, would have seemed completely inappropriate. But nobody liked Rob. I couldn't think of anyone who worked on the set because they wanted to, including the actors. Syndication was the magic word. That's what we were going for. But work dissatisfaction was hardly a murder motive. I mean, if you don't like your job, you can always quit—which I now realized I should have done a long time ago. Go back to waiting tables.

"He's made enemies," I conceded. "But not in the sense of someone wanting to kill him. We've had the usual contract disputes, disgruntled technical staff... Really, nothing that could push someone over the edge like this." Honestly, the only loose cannon I could think of was Frank. Good thing he'd been with me at the station all night.

Hail rubbed his sunburned arm. "There was nothing out of the ordinary lately?"

The contest, it hit me. Rob had claimed something was fishy in one of the entries. But, again, this was Rob. Any stupid little press junket was a "media event." Story lines we had recycled from the previous seasons were "dramatic new developments." Yet, I felt compelled to point out the contest.

"Yes, yes, I've heard about it." Hail nodded, proving, once again, that publicity worked. "Interesting idea. Very interesting."

"Yeah, well, Rob thought we needed something new. Competition's stiff, and it gave us that edge." I yawned, somehow discrediting that last statement. Who was I kidding, our show was a yawn. A couple more years to syndication. Syndication. I wondered if we had lost it now with Rob's death. Just how brainwashed had I become? Here we were—with Rob found murdered—and I was still thinking about syndication.

"About that contest," I finally said, "Rob was convinced—I'd say almost obsessed—with the idea of finding something sensational in the entries. We had narrowed it down to four finalists. And every night I found him back at his desk going over their stories. He said he was working on a real bombshell." There, I'd said it. Not that I was convinced there was anything to it. But at least I was cooperating. And that's all I felt I could do with my head pounding after another sleepless night.

Trish Grady

For Corinne, Michael and me it was déjà vu. Here we were again, at the police station answering questions. But this time we were dealing with murder. Cold-blooded, horrifying murder. And—with the exception of Michael—this was definitely new territory. I was scared. Could one of us be next? Jeremy assured me that Rob had been targeted. He had made one too many enemies in the business. Probably jealousy, I could see that. But what I found most disconcerting—and telling!—was the complete lack of concern from the crew. A successful, charming Hollywood director brutally stabbed, and they simply went on, unfazed by this minor interruption. Rob was quickly replaced by his assistant director Garth, a convenient understudy already in place. Why didn't anyone focus on this guy? That's one heck of a career jump, from assistant to director overnight! And I didn't like him, no, not one bit. The tight-lipped accountant type with nerdy round glasses and a high-pitched voice when he called for "Action!" He was nothing like Rob, who had oozed charm and success. After all, he had built *Crystal Falls* into the successful show it had become. But how quickly people forget.

I felt awful and useless. I had nothing to contribute to the investigation. I had watched a rerun of *The Apprentice*, then some far too violent movie with Antonio Banderas in it. And none of the others had joined me. I didn't blame them. After all, we were competitors. This was not the time to get chummy. To be honest, they weren't my type of crowd to begin with. We had nothing in common. And to be even more blunt, I found them a highly ungrateful bunch. But I would only tell you that. And my diary. Just think, after all that trouble the producers went through, putting us up in that beautiful mansion … We had an indoor and outdoor pool! But not an ounce of gratitude from any of them. Corinne was obviously just here for the cash. She was nothing but a gold digger. And I suspected so was Michael. Though hadn't he collected a nice insurance payout after his wife died? All too convenient, if you asked me. He seemed to know an awful lot of people. He probably got off using one of his connections. Even here, he was always talking on the phone. Mainly to some guy named Julian, who I'd learned was his former business partner.

And then there was that Stephen guy. Don't even get me started on him! I mean, why would you want to be on a show that you, admittedly, had never watched and had absolutely no interest in? Just by the way he was always fidgeting, you could tell this guy was hiding something. His wife sounded sweet though. What a jerk he was, not going with her to those wig fittings. And then immediately after her death hitting on that sales woman. The nerve! He was probably already cheating on her during the marriage. Men.

I vented all my anger and frustrations—and, of course, my complete shock and dismay about Rob's horrible death!—in my diary. I must say it felt liberating. I hadn't kept a diary in a really long time. I used to, back in my teens when we all did it. I guess kids still do, only now they call it blogging. And it's not private anymore. Yeah, like anyone is really interested. But kids are so naïve. They actually believe people care what they think. Well, you cared about my thoughts, obviously. That's why you asked for my point of view. And I appreciated the opportunity to tell you my side. Even though I knew I couldn't be of much help.

* * * *

Michael Palmer

Yes, I immediately hired a lawyer. I had been through the legal system before, and this time, wanted to make sure I was adequately represented. Even when no one openly declared me a suspect.

Of course I was shocked by Rob's death. Both by the untimeliness and the violent nature of his demise. But I've learned there is no correct way of responding to the unthinkable. If the suspect acts emotional, he is definitely covering up. If he appears calm and composed, he is perceived as callous and calculating. Maybe even cruel enough to…

I was not proud of it, but upon hearing the news, my primary concern was me. What was supposed to be my ticket out had landed me right in the middle of another murder investigation.

None of us contestants had a decent alibi. I knew that didn't look good. We were in Hollywood and hadn't left our rooms. Something had to be wrong with us just for that. Man, how I wished I had joined Trish, that obnoxious housewife, in the living room that night. No wonder her husband had cheated. I probably would have been speeding away too, had I noticed some hysterical old hag chasing me.

Jeremy told us someone had taken off with the two hundred grand. Any of us contestants or crew members could have stolen the money. Stupid idea, anyway. Why keep the two hundred grand around in cash? Because it looks better on TV, that's why. The winner opens the suitcase and there's the big kahuna. Not a tiny paper check stuffed in an envelope. And the producers hadn't learned a thing from Rob's death and the subsequent theft. The missing cash was quickly replaced with—you guessed it!—more cash. You should have seen the relief in Corinne's eyes.

The film crew made a really big deal of it too. The executive producer himself—who, up to this point, had never bothered showing his face—came out and presented the newly filled suitcase. I initially found it tacky and tasteless, considering a man had lost his life. Then it dawned on me: this was nothing but bait for the prime suspects. I started doubting that the guy really was one of the producers. Much more likely an undercover cop.

I wondered if the money alone was enough of a motive, though. True, two hundred grand was a nice payday. But, let's face it, that Rob guy was a jerk. There probably was no shortage of suspects. And yet, I noted with some anger, fingers were, once again, pointed at me. Why would I possibly have killed Rob? I came here to clear my name. I would have entered the contest had no money been involved. And yes, you could hook me up to the lie detector for that one. But I was getting agitated, and my lawyer had advised me not to show too much emotion. I would proceed with cautious cooperation. I would not even opt out of the reality shoot. And I would stay the additional two weeks the police had requested. Whatever it took to lift that cloud of suspicion.

Corinne Prichett

Michael was convinced we were all suspects. I thought he was paranoid. Why would any of us have murdered Rob? After all, we stood something to gain here—two hundred grand! Why would we have jeopardized all that? Yes, I'll admit, at first I was worried. I had come so far. Did this mean the contest was over? I knew it was selfish. Rob was dead, and here I was only thinking about the money. But I needed it more than anyone. I was sure of that.

I was relieved when they told us that the contest was still on. The assistant director, a guy named Garth, took over for Rob. I felt sorry for that Garth guy. He seemed to be in way over his head. He was nervous. Even I could tell, and I had never been to a soap shoot before. Nobody took Garth seriously just because he was a decent guy, not a sleazebag like Rob. He was actually trying to put out a good show, not chase skirts. Yet the crew ignored him, while the actors insisted they had a better understanding of their characters. After all, he was just the director.

Jeremy was officially in charge of that stupid reality shoot now. Yep, another guy to feel sorry for. The producers were even making him move in with us. We had all been asked to stay an additional two weeks to facilitate the police investigation. Frankly, I didn't care. It was not like I had anyplace else to go.

Michael immediately hired a lawyer. I didn't understand why he was so convinced that we, the contestants, were the main suspects. Personally, I would have focused on the crew. They all knew about the prize and where the money was. And I didn't see how anybody could have spent a significant amount of time around Rob without wanting to kill him. He was one of the most repellant individuals I'd ever met. I realize that might be shocking for you to hear, but you said you wanted the truth. If I had known Rob before, I might very well have reconsidered entering this contest. Tellingly, no one seemed to miss him, either. Only Trish was beside herself about what had happened. She kept checking the paper, going on and on about how none of the articles painted Rob in a good enough light. She said someone needed to put out a real obituary for him. The kind they wrote for ordinary people, not a bunch of media hype. An obituary? That was the least of our problems right now. But if you asked me, I thought it was all an act. Two hundred grand was a pretty good reason to fake compassion. I wished I was better at it myself.

At times I did wonder what we looked like, four people with no alibis. We had spent the night of the murder in our rooms. Yeah, right. But what else were we supposed to do? It's not like we knew anybody in LA. Besides, they dragged us all over the set each day. I enjoyed having some peace and quiet at night. They couldn't honestly expect us to hang out together. Trish was annoying—one of the few things we could all agree on. Stephen was okay, if a bit strange. He couldn't sit still for five minutes and was always searching through his pockets. But whenever someone offered him a light, he insisted he had quit smoking. He could actually say that and keep a straight face. Though we had all seen him light up. More than once. And Michael… well, I wasn't sure if he had done anything wrong. But the whole circumstances surrounding his wife's death were pretty creepy. And what was he doing here, anyway? Her life insurance payout should have been a couple hundred grand right there. He was probably set. So what did he have to be on TV for?

Now Trish, I could see. She was just the kind of person that would want her fifteen minutes. Not that she had anything to say. But then lots of folks didn't, and they all got their fifteen minutes. And Stephen, well, he really wanted fifteen minutes for a loved one. Which was kinda sweet, but useless nonetheless. No, as far as I was concerned, money was the only valid motivation here. At least I was honest about it. Let the others complain that I was greedy. And I knew they had plenty to say about me! For two hundred grand I could live with all that. At least for a couple more weeks.

* * * *

Stephen Dowell

Two extra weeks. Man, I hoped Irene could see me up there. Yes, I promised I would stay the extra time. 'Cause that's how much she meant to me.

I just wished I could smoke. I had never needed a smoke so badly in my life. But I couldn't even do that. All for you, Jillian. I didn't even know why I was bothering anymore. I wanted to do something right in my life for once, I guess. I promised to quit smoking, so I would. Not that she was there to see it. But I wanted to prove to her that I wasn't scum. That I could keep my promises. Though I wasn't even buying it myself. I was scum. Of course she didn't want to see me anymore.

I wondered if anyone would care if I were found dead. Nobody seemed to care about that Rob guy. Trish maybe. She seemed to dig his oily charm. That other girl, Corinne, was too aloof. Good for her.

Michael said we should all get lawyers. I couldn't see why. I thought only suspects got lawyers. And only once they'd been charged. Well, maybe Michael had good reason to expect to be charged any minute. But the rest of us? Why bother?

Believe it or not, I was not even enjoying the mansion. I felt like a homeless person sleeping on a mattress for the first time. Their back might kill them in the morning, but society dictates that's what life was supposed to be like. Shut up and be happy. These days I found myself wishing I was back at the warehouse.

I did all this for Irene. I wanted to get her a part on that show. I knew it would have meant the world. But here I was, and all they were interested in was me. The guy that cheated on her in death and screwed things up with Jillian right after. I didn't want to be part of this. I didn't need to see myself on TV. I was nothing like Trish or Michael. Now Corinne was different. She was just here for the money. Fair enough. Nothing wrong with that.

I grew up poor, I knew what it was like. And she was young. She could use the money to go back to school and get a decent job. She didn't belong in a warehouse. It was probably the best way to use that money. Irene would have agreed with that. Though I secretly suspected Trish to be the front-runner. Not that I was an expert on these sort of things. But Trish kept saying how her story was the most soap-like. She was probably right. She struck me as the kind of person that watches soaps all day. What I would have hated most was for Michael to win. Wasn't it enough to cash in on his dead wife's life insurance? Well, alright, so did I. But I didn't kill her. Big difference. Which brought me back to that Rob guy. No shortage of suspects there, if you asked me.

Someone, obviously, was after that money. But other motives could have played a part. The way Rob was hitting on Corinne… come on, that was borderline harassment! And probably not the first time he'd been guilty of that. If I were a woman, I probably would have grabbed the nearest fire extinguisher, too.

The new guy, Garth, told us Jeremy would be moving in with us. Easier with that reality shoot and all. I didn't mind. Anything to get this over with faster. Besides, we had plenty of room here, and Trish had been yakking our ears off. Let someone else put up with that for a while. Wondered why they picked Jeremy, though. The kid obviously had no experience and seemed even less enthused than the rest of us.

Man, I really needed a smoke. Sorry, Jill.

* * * *

Jeremy Lawren

Not that I would have admitted it back then, but something about Detective Hail just pushed my buttons. He was about my age. A young guy, and not even particularly athletic looking. And still, he had managed to get into the police force. He was doing something with his life. Something meaningful. He was fighting crime, while I had spent the past three years of my life doing what exactly? So when he pointed out the part about there being "certain risks" involved sharing such close quarters with the suspects, I couldn't say no. It was as simple as that.

So I took up residence with them the next day, officially there to produce something like a reality show starring our final four contestants. I'm not sure they believed it. Well, I'm pretty sure Michael didn't. Can't say I blamed him.

They didn't seem thrilled to have me around. But for now, my roommates showed reluctant cooperation. I did my best to put them at ease. The audience wanted to get to know them, and we had made a promise to the owner to feature the mansion. Plus, it would be great publicity for our show, which we definitely needed after all the negative coverage we had gotten out of Rob's death. I had laid out every bogus reason and garnered little more than a few polite nods and suspicious stares from Michael.

That "behind the scenes" footage shoot would have been a hurdle even under less stressful conditions. But the added complication of a murder was the last thing we needed. They weren't actors, not even reality show contestants. We had sprung the idea of filming at the mansion on them at the last minute. Big mistake. Not one of them was comfortable in front of the camera. And I wasn't behind it, either! Let me say this once and for all: not everyone wants to direct! And if reality shows were one of the categories considered for Razzies, we'd be cleaning up that year.

"Don't we need someone to do our make-up?" Trish pouted. "You can't expect us to go in front of the camera like that!"

"I'm not puttin' on any make-up," Stephen declared loudly. "Forget it."

"I didn't mean lipstick," Trish snapped back. "But at least a decent foundation. I don't wanna have my face look all shiny. Corinne, you tell them."

"Why me?"

"You worked at a spa!"

"I'm with Stephen," Michael said solemnly. "I'm not getting dolled up for this."

I turned to Trish. "If you would like to put on some make-up, go right ahead. But the idea, the vision we had for this is an honest, intimate look at the contestants. Something the audience can relate to." The vision we had... I almost choked on my own words. The vision we had was to rip off your sob stories, get some publicity, and stay on air for a couple more seasons.

"Let's start out with each of you introducing yourself..."

"But we've already done that," Trish objected.

"Yes," I conceded, "but that was your first time in front of the camera. Everybody was a little stiff then, so I suggest we take another shot at this."

"You suggest?" Corinne arched an eyebrow. "I thought you were the director. That's not much of a direction."

"Alright," I said, clearly fed up with the attitudes. "I demand you introduce yourselves. Happy?"

"May I suggest we stop this bickering nonsense?" Michael intervened. "If we want to get this over with, you guys need to cooperate. Tell the audience a bit about yourselves. Where you're from, what you do and what drew you to *Crystal Falls* in the first place."

"Nothing ever drew me to *Crystal Falls*," Stephen threw in unhelpfully.

"Yes, and we all know it by now," Trish snapped at him. "You're like a broken record."

"Maybe we can start out by shooting a complete tour of the mansion," Michael suggested. "Let's show how we've been accommodated by the producers. You know, express our gratitude and appreciation." He was annoying me now, the way he was taking over. Those should have been my suggestions, with me being the director and all. Ah well. We had to start somewhere. Maybe showing off the mansion wasn't a bad way to ease everybody in. It would make a good filler, anyway. And boy, did we need some fillers! This crowd would hardly yield a first act.

Besides, I reasoned, Michael had to feel in charge. Being suspicious of people was second nature to him. Had I objected, he would have immediately interpreted it as mistrust on my part. The police had instructed me to appear as non-threatening as possible. Let them think I'm the young, naïve kid, in way over his head. They were more likely to open up to me that way. I had to keep telling myself it was for the best because, well, I actually wanted to be in charge. I wanted to do a good job. I had wasted the past three years doing menial tasks. I just had to keep reminding myself that my real challenge here was to nail the prime suspect, not make my small screen directorial debut.

Lying in bed that night, I kept going over Rob's death. My gut instinct pointed at Trish. Rob had been hinting at how she may not be telling the whole truth about her part in the accident. And come to think of it, she had immediately reacted alarmed when I'd mentioned our legal team would want us to verify their stories. Which wasn't even true. That was just me stalling for time. But now I was kicking myself. What did I have to say that for? The last thing I wanted was to raise an alarm!

And of course, she acted the most upset about Rob's murder, though she had hardly gotten to know him in the brief time the contestants had spent here. She even produced some real tears! That would have been a stretch for our actors! But why was she assuming the role of a close relative? It was just plain creepy.

Besides, nobody could prove Trish had spent the evening in front of the TV. What if she had taken off? She could have made her way over to Skyview. It was entirely possible, seeing we had generously provided them with rental cars.

Stupid, stupid me, running my mouth about the legal department and the background checks. Maybe my dumb remark led to the murder. I should have mentioned it to the investigators. Yeah, I probably should have.

* * * *

Corinne Prichett

I wish I had been a bit nicer to Jeremy when they made him move in with us. We were all on edge, but that was no excuse. None of it was his fault, anyway. And here, they'd thrown him right into the lion's den. The four of us didn't get along. By then it was painfully obvious. We were all increasingly annoyed with Michael for putting himself in charge of everything. He made endless observations about the lighting. He determined which room to shoot in at what time of day, and even insisted we needed a second camera at the mansion. We didn't even have enough material for one camera, let alone two! So he had a bit of experience in graphics. Big deal. May I remind everyone that his business went bust? I felt bad for his brother-in-law, who probably never got to make a single decision. Ironically, Michael spent a lot of time on the phone with the guy now. Mainly complaining about the rest of us, of course.

Jeremy seemed to take Michael's antics in stride. Maybe he realized he had no other option if he wanted any footage at all. Couldn't they just have paid for the mansion instead of shilling for it with some reality freak show? Who would want to rent if after that?

"Hey." I approached Jeremy one night.

He was sitting alone by the pool, reading some sports magazine. "Pro tips for mountain bikers." He was probably wishing himself far, far away. He looked up, squinting against the evening sun.

"What's up?"

"Nothing. Just trying to get away from Trish for a while." I smiled. I wasn't sure if he would mind my company. He'd probably had enough of us by now. I couldn't blame him. I had had enough of us.

But he moved some papers from the chair beside him to make room for me. "So, I take it this is your first film project." Good one, Corinne. Insult the guy right off the bat.

He smiled. "That obvious, huh?"

"I'm afraid we're not the easiest bunch to work with."

"Well, it looks like Michael's got it under control," he said, resigned and amused at the same time.

"Can I ask you something?" I said. "Why are you doing this?"

"Doing what?"

"The shoot here at the mansion. Why did you accept to be in charge of that? I don't think you're having a very good time with it. Couldn't you just say no?" I surprised myself being so blunt. But it was just the two of us, alone by the pool. I figured he'd be honest with me.

"It's the least I can do for Rob now," he simply said. "I owe him that much."

I nodded, not entirely convinced. "So he was a good friend of yours then?"

"I wouldn't say friend," he conceded. "You met Rob. He wasn't the easiest guy to get along with. But he gave me an enormous opportunity here. And I owe him for that."

I sat beside him in one of the empty lawn chairs. A nice warm breeze blew even at that time of the day. Jeremy probably didn't notice. But being from Toronto, I did.

"You have any idea who wanted him dead?" I asked.

Jeremy shook his head. "I don't think the police have any clues yet either."

"Does that scare you?" I don't know why I asked. Maybe because it scared me at times.

"Why would it?" He looked at me, an odd mix of surprise and defiance in his eyes.

"Well," I pointed out cautiously, "if they have no clues yet, you don't know if it had something to do with Rob personally or if it was related to the show. Or even the contest. In that case, any one of us could be next. It could be you. Or me."

"Why would it be related to the show?" He seemed annoyed now. Maybe he thought I was getting paranoid like Michael. "No, Rob was a tough guy. He probably made one too many enemies. Which I doubt I have. So, no, I don't think I'll be next."

I nodded, thought I didn't quite believe him. His boss got murdered. He had to be a little apprehensive, at least. Unless he himself... no, nonsense. Though he was the last to see Rob alive. For a moment I felt uncomfortable sitting there alone with him. Now I was definitely getting paranoid. Enough of that. He was at the police station that night. Which was more of an alibi than the rest of us could produce.

"So why does nobody really care about Rob's death?" I asked, realizing too late what a bold statement that was.

"You think nobody cares?" he asked, raising an eyebrow.

"Well, with the exception of Trish, maybe. Personally, I think she's putting on a big show."

"You think I don't care?"

"I'm sorry." I grabbed his arm. "That came out wrong. I didn't mean to imply you didn't care. It's just the rest of the crew—"

It was at that moment that Trish chose to join us.

"Hey guys, enjoying the evening sun?"

* * * *

Trish Grady

I didn't trust her from the start. That little flirt. First she played all hard to get with Rob. And now she had moved on to Jeremy. I saw it. She was even spending time alone with him by the pool. Of the four of us, she had gone through the least. She knew her story was the weakest and was simply trying to win by seducing the crew. But you couldn't trust her, that little liar. Just think about it. Who keeps something as personal and precious as an engagement ring? With no regard for the woman who lost it? And yet, she did it with such a sense of entitlement. After all, she was poor, poor Corinne, and life owed her, right? Nonsense. She had her whole life ahead of her. No kids, no jailbird husband, no obligations. Couldn't she see that? Some day some poor unsuspecting guy would fall for her, not realizing the total lack of character behind that pretty little façade. But I would make sure that guy would not be Jeremy. You don't win that easily, hun. No, I would not be cheated out of my win by that little floozy. Why did there always have to be another woman? Didn't honesty count for anything anymore? I had told the truth about my husband. At my own expense, at my children's. But that little liar…

And she despised me, I could tell. She had sized me up from the start, and concluded this would be an easy win. It's always about looks, isn't it? If I hadn't been an overweight, out-of-shape housewife with drab hair and thin lips… My husband would never have cheated on me, and Christopher Berndt would not be a quadriplegic. People believe that. On bad days, I do myself.

I had tried to visit him in the hospital, you know. I'd felt it would make things, well, not right. Things would never be right again. Not for him, not for me. They'd told him he would never walk again. And my family lay in ruins. But something…

So I went up to his hospital room. But I never got past the introduction. As soon as I told him who I was, he totally freaked out. He started yelling profanities. Two nurses finally came and escorted me out. This was all my fault. My fault for being a boring old hag whose husband just had to get away from her.

* * * *

Michael Palmer

Why wouldn't the others cooperate? Why make the shoot so difficult? Clearly none of us wanted to be here, so the sooner we got this over with, the better. Were they too dense to see that?

Yes, maybe I overstepped the boundaries a little by putting myself in charge. But someone had to be, and Jeremy... well, let's just say he wasn't.

What puzzled me most was that the others couldn't see how important this shoot was. Couldn't they tell we were all suspects? This was our one and only opportunity to show how we were just innocent people caught in a dreadful situation. At the very least they should have been thankful for the exposure. The whole point was to be on TV, right? Wasn't that why they entered the contest? Well then, for those who didn't win, the reality show would at least provide some sort of consolation prize. I must admit—though I was careful never to voice it out loud—I was certain I would take first place. How could any of them even come close? No, not in light of what I had been through those last couple of years.

Maybe that's why I needed to direct this in the first place. I was tired of being censored by my lawyers. I needed to be in charge of my own life again.

Of the three of them, Trish gave me the most to work with. Okay, we would have to edit out some useless sections. Like her ten minute rant about Ivy's varying hairstyles and why none of them had worked. And yes, we'd have to tone it down a bit. She was a drama queen. Let's face it, the husband—while incarcerated—was still very much alive. The person most hurt in all this was that poor quadriplegic guy. And he wasn't even related.

I was most disappointed with Corinne. The girl completely failed to see the chance she was given. She was pretty. This could have led to bigger things for her. You'd think someone as poor as her would have jumped on that. Granted, she probably didn't stand a chance as an actress. She was far too stiff in front of the camera and never cracked a smile. But I'm sure she could have done some catalogue work, at least. It had to be a step up from the gummy factory. But that's what's wrong with young folks today. They lack ambition. They want everything handed to them on a platter. And that Jeremy kid was no better. He would never make it as a director.

Now Stephen… to call the guy uncooperative would have been the understatement of the year. I caught him smoking—on camera!—more than a few times. So he was cheesed with me after that—yeah, like he was fooling any of us before! One morning he pantsed me as I was about to go for an early swim—also, on camera. I am sorry to say this escalated into a fight, during which both of us—and the camera—ended up in the pool, handily destroying the evidence. Unfortunately, the camera was toast, too. We somehow talked Jeremy into accepting the blame.

Jeremy Lawren

I never did take responsibility for that camera, though it was convenient to let the guys think so. Now they owed me. Especially Stephen. Man, did that guy have a temper! Scary. I wish he'd just resume smoking. Without his nicotine, the guy was a ticking time bomb.

Of the four of them, I could picture Stephen being Rob's killer most easily. Mainly because I could see him putting in the necessary force into swinging that fire extinguisher. And he evidently had a really short fuse.

I went to talk to Garth about a replacement camera, half-wondering how I was going to explain that one. But as it turned out, I didn't need to explain anything at all. When I got to the set, Garth, looking a good three shades paler than usual, was arguing with some insurance guy that something—despite the apparent level of stupidity involved—still qualified as an "accidental fire." Thus, it should be fully covered. It turned out that during one of the shoots someone had actually kindled a fire in Jake and Ivy's mock fireplace for a more realistic look. Yep, we got some brilliant minds on this show! This, unfortunately, had spread very quickly to the mostly mock—and cheap—furniture. What hadn't been destroyed in the not-so-mock fire got completely soaked by the sprinklers.

Garth, understandably, couldn't care less about the whens and hows of my request for a second camera. It would be sent out to the mansion later that afternoon. Unfortunately, it wouldn't be the last camera destroyed in the process.

* * * *

Stephen Dowell

When they first told us Rob had been murdered, I wondered who was capable of such a thing. But now I had changed my mind. After almost two weeks under the same roof with Michael, I had concluded we were all capable of murder. Even me. Under the right circumstances, that is. But hey, whoever dunnit certainly had the circumstances lined up right. So far there were no suspects—apart from everyone who ever had to deal with Rob! Nothing to go on. According to Jeremy, the investigation now focused on that stupid set fire. Just 'cause some genius thought you could light up a mock fireplace.

I apologized to Jeremy for that whole camera incident. It was completely Michael's fault anyway, with him freaking out like that. Besides, he was shoving that thing in our faces all day long. Even when we were eating or on the phone, trying to make a personal call. Never any privacy. He also claimed to have lots of footage of me smoking. But that was just baloney. None of his business, anyway.

It bothered me when he wouldn't leave me alone. Yeah, I was trying to call her, so what? See if she'd talk to me. And there he was with that stupid camera again. She hung up on me. There, happy? She thinks I'm a total lowlife, having lied about my dead wife. But it's not like I killed her, okay? Which was more than one could say with certainty about Michael. And that's why I never thought he could win this contest. 'Cause if he hadn't killed his wife, well, fair enough if he wanted to tell his side of the story. Problem was, his story didn't have an ending. I don't watch much TV, and I'm no expert. But I would assume the audience—like the rest of us—would want an explanation how the wife died. Something he himself claimed not to know the answer to. Well, I had my own theory. According to his lawyer, there were only two possibilities: murder or accidental death. But here's the thing: what if his wife had tried to push him over that balcony, and really, who could have blamed her? Then he acted in self-defense or whatever you call it. But he flat-out denied having anything to do with it. He got off on a pure technicality. Not enough evidence leaves "reasonable doubt."

Funny though how quick he himself was to point fingers. That morning he couldn't find his laptop and immediately accused me of being a thief. But why would I be interested in his stupid computer with his dumb notes? Frankly, I think he made the whole thing up.

* * * *

Trish Grady

No, I didn't take that laptop. Of course that didn't stop Michael from accusing every single one of us as we were clearly out to get him. Things got particularly ugly between him and Stephen. They were both such hotheads! I wouldn't want to tick either of them off. Maybe that's what Rob had done. I could be living under one roof with the murderer!

The tension in the house was rising. I got increasingly concerned about my own safety. I had kids. Kids whose father was in prison. They needed at least one parent to come home. I had to make it out of here alive. So I suggested we have a barbecue.

That's right, a barbecue. We would all hang out together. With the camera off, we agreed. Then we would prove we could act civilized for one evening. Besides, I reasoned, my chances of getting murdered were severely diminished with a crowd around. We had agreed to meet by the outdoor pool around seven. I had even dressed up a bit to show I was making an effort.

"My neighbor used to have one of these patio tables," I said, gliding my hand across the checkered top. "You can put a cigarette out on this material, and it won't burn." I knew nobody cared. I really just said it to make conversation.

Michael rolled his eyes. "When on earth would you ever need that?"

Stephen immediately got out his lighter.

Michael sighed. "See what you've done! Don't give this guy ideas."

"Chicken or beef?" Jeremy asked a little too cheerfully, wiping his hands on his Kiss-the-Cook apron.

"I'll have one of each," I replied. "This looks delicious."

"Chicken for me," Corinne announced, kissing Jeremy on the cheek. I tried my best to ignore her.

"I'll take whatever," Stephen grumbled. "As long as I don't have to kiss you."

* * * *

Corinne Prichett

Yes, I kissed Jeremy. I did it purely to bug her. It was innocent enough, just a little peck on the cheek. I wasn't so stupid as to hit on him and get disqualified.

I'm a hard worker, okay? I am not lazy, despite what Trish and Michael were insinuating. I had overheard them more than a few times, especially when Jeremy was around. They went on and on about how I had my whole life ahead of me and simply wasn't doing enough to get out of poverty. I didn't have the money to go to college. Was that so hard to understand?

And what about those two, while we were at it? Both had been conveniently living off their spouses. Trish never had to work. And Michael had been relying on his wife's income for years, too proud to admit he didn't know the first thing about running a business. Even having fallen flat on his face, he still wasn't coming off his high horse. He immediately had to appoint himself director. Like his bit of graphics experience made him some kind of expert. And now he was up in arms about his missing laptop. Like any of us were dying to read his notes.

"For the last time," he declared between bites, "whoever took it, just leave it on the kitchen counter. No questions asked."

"What was on there," Stephen teased, "your confession?"

"That's not funny."

Trish gasped. "Are you saying Michael killed his wife?"

"I'm not saying anything. But with the laptop gone and him causing such a stink about it, kinda makes you wonder what was on there."

"My outline for our reality project. That's what, jerk."

"Our project?" I threw in. "It's not like any of us have a say in it. You act like it's yours and yours only. Like you're the only one with ideas!"

He sneered back. "You don't have any ideas. You need an original thought once in a while, honey. Something other than woe-is-me."

Trish immediately sided with him. "You think life owes you."

"Why would I think that," I said. "'Cause I'm busting my butt off in a factory instead of sitting on my big fat ass, watching

Crystal Falls, waiting for my husband to bring home the pay?" The gloves were off now. "The question is not why your husband joined the gym. It's why didn't you?"

"Guys!" Jeremy frantically signaled the time out sign. "And gals... First of all, what's wrong with watching *Crystal Falls*? It's quality entertainment programming," he added, a tad too sarcastically.

"Ah, look at you! Going for employee of the month again." Stephen cracked open a beer. I thought he had given up drinking. Probably the same way he had given up smoking.

"Pass me one, too." Jeremy held out his hand.

"No can do." Stephen shook his head. "'Cause, technically, you're still on the job. So I don't think you're allowed to drink."

"And technically, you're a recovering alcoholic," Michael threw back at him. "So I don't think you—"

I was waiting for Stephen to punch him—or at least throw the beer in his face—and was surprised when he didn't.

"I'm not an alcoholic," he said, and it almost sounded sad.

"Oops, you just skipped step one." Michael sneered. "That is step one—admitting you're an alcoholic—right?"

"As you should know from Control Freaks Anonymous," I replied. His constant remarks about Stephen were utterly annoying. Michael had no proof the guy ever had a drinking problem. But he was quick to jump to conclusions 'cause Stephen worked in a warehouse. Of course, us blue collar workers were all uneducated, lazy booze hounds.

"So far Michael's been the only one to come up with some ideas. All you guys do is criticize," Trish threw in, obviously just kissing up to Michael. She had probably concluded he was the least competition. The producers couldn't crown a suspected murderer the winner. The press would be all over that. Then again, maybe that's exactly what they were going for.

"Okay, here's what I've come up with," I blurted out. It was a bold statement. Honestly, I was making this up as I went. "We will do interviews, one-on-one. Jeremy, you can stay in charge of the camera. That way Garth doesn't have to spare anyone else. Poor guy has enough to do on the set. So... we'll pick pairs... like, Trish and Michael, me and Stephen. We'll interview each other—all questions are permitted. And then we'll switch sides."

My suggestion was greeted by a stunned silence. Maybe they were each weighing the pros and cons of that approach. I was a little taken aback myself. I actually liked my idea. There was an original thought in my head, after all.

* * * *

Jeremy Lawren

I was not convinced this would work, but opted not to say anything. At least Corinne's plan shut them up for a while. That alone was worth trying the one-on-one talks. I'd had enough of their fighting for one night. And even if the interviews would yield more of the same—bickering, mistrust, competitors tearing each other apart with the tape rolling—we would at least be filming something. In the end, I would dutifully hand the tapes over to the police and let them draw their own conclusions. Who knows, maybe they would catch one of the contestants in a lie. Maybe it would give them that elusive angle to pursue in this investigation.

I wanted to start the next morning, just to show the cops I could handle this. No need to send someone in undercover. The less crew around, the more likely the suspects were to open up. Corinne would go on camera first. The others had, of course, nailed her on that. She picked Stephen—the only one who hadn't been openly hostile towards her—as her interviewer.

We set up in the living room, her choice location. Michael and Trish hovered over my shoulder as I positioned the camera.

"Guys," I finally said, "give us some space, will you? I think we should keep it to one interviewer and their partner. The rest of you, take some time off. Go for a swim."

"After all, it's safe now," Corinne said to Michael sarcastically. "Stephen's here with me. You can keep your pants on. Not that we'd ever wanna see that again."

"Like your bony butt would be so much better," Trish snapped at her.

"Enough," I yelled, not waiting for the inevitable remark about Trish's behind. I got everyone to agree that, from now on, we would all keep our pants on in shared spaces. Then I sent Trish and Michael on their way. I had to. Nothing else would work. I would never catch any one of them unguarded with the others watching.

Trish pouted and turned around. Michael grumbled some condescending remark I could easily have taken personally. But they finally both took off.

* * * *

91

Stephen Dowell

I didn't wanna do this, but couldn't think of any other way to finally get this shoot over with.

"Why'd ya have to pick me?" was, hence, my first question.

"You seem like the nicest of the bunch." Corinne batted her pretty blue eyes at me.

I nodded. "Trying to butter me up. It's working. So, how do you like LA?"

"I like it. I like the weather and this." She motioned across the room. "This is a huge step up from how I live. It's got furniture."

"So what would you do with the money should you win?" *And what would you do to win?* I added silently. *Murder someone?* Naw, she was way too small to swing that fire extinguisher.

"Buy some furniture. And I'd go to college," she said without hesitation. "Maybe even study overseas. Believe it or not, this is my first time out of Ontario. Pretty pathetic, huh? I'd love to go to Europe, even just for a short while. You miss Scotland?"

"I've been here for a while now."

"Ever been back? You still got family over there?"

"I have but… Hey, it's my turn to ask the questions. So, what's wrong with Ontario?"

"I dunno. Nothing, I guess. But I grew up in a single parent household. We never had any money. I never felt like I was part of the crowd, if you know what I mean."

"You think your friends cared you didn't have money?"

"I never really got to make friends, hang out, you know. We were living in Guelph, with this old aunt of mine. Well, she wasn't a real aunt, but we had to call her that. She supported herself by giving piano lessons. So we always had to keep real quiet around the house. I couldn't bring people over. So I read a lot. Especially about faraway places. I always pictured growing up somewhere else. Things would be so different."

I almost laughed. I grew up in the infamous Castlemilk Housing Scheme. Surrounded by drunks and addicts and refugees who probably second-guessed their decision to flee to Scotland. Where they came from couldn't have been that bad. Our front door didn't even have glass in it. Somebody had shoved a piece of plywood in its place, which somehow made it worse. It made it official. There was no point replacing the glass 'cause things would never change.

What I wouldn't have given for some peace and quiet every once in a while. Even with a piano-playing fake aunt.

"Can I ask you something?"

"You're the interviewer. Asking me something would be part of your job." She smiled sarcastically, but her tone wasn't as mean as when she talked to Michael.

"Why didn't you just sell the ring? Get some nice furniture or go on that trip to Europe. Why keep the thing? It didn't do you any good."

"Pretty stupid, huh?" She turned her head away, and I was sorry I'd asked. I knew. She had kept it because it made her feel special. Just like Irene with that wig. And I was too dumb to see it then, too.

"So, did you take Michael's laptop?" I asked, in an effort to lighten the mood.

"No." She looked at me a little offended, but then slowly smiled when she realized I'd been joking. "But I would like to express my sincere gratitude to whoever did. Any further questions?"

Corinne Prichett

"Have you quit smoking?" I started with that one, just to see what level of honesty I was going to get here.

"Yes."

The look on my face must have made it clear that I didn't believe him.

"Look," he said, "I used to smoke, well, maybe between sixty and seventy-five cigarettes a day. Now I'm down to fifteen. So, I've quit smoking at least forty-five."

How could I argue with that kind of logic?

"So, what would you do with the money?" I asked instead. *And would you kill for it?*

Stephen yawned. "Why'd we have to do this so early in the morning? Okay, let's see... I'd buy you a ticket to Scotland. Show you some of our finest public housing. Just so you'd count your blessings to not have grown up there. Satisfied?"

I pictured rows of little red brickstone houses, kind of like you see on *Coronation Street*. He laughed out loud. "Nooo, noooo... those are mansions, compared. I'm talking ugly, run-down, cheap tarrazo."

I didn't know what that was and made the grave mistake of asking. You do not get Stephen started about building materials.

"It's not your traditional stone construction. They built these things just after the Second World War, and that would've been too expensive. You make terrazzo facings by setting marble chips into cement, and then polishing the surface and—"

Jeremy threw me an exasperated look, clearly not interested in Glasgow's low-income housing.

"But at least everyone around you was poor, too," I quickly threw in. "You didn't have to feel like an outsider. You had your own community."

Stephen looked at me like I was mad. "Now I'm definitely gonna buy you that ticket, girl. Look, there's nothing romantic about being poor. It sucks either way. And community?" He sneered and shook his head. "No, it's not. You're just surrounded by drunks and addicts and lots of folks who don't speak English.

How's that a community? Poverty sucks, okay? So let's not form a club around it."

"But you got out," I said.

"Ah, yeah. That was always the plan. You have to get out, you know."

"Is that why you married Irene? To get out?"

"Nooo," he objected, sounding awfully hurt. I was immediately sorry it had come out that way. "How can you even think that? If I just wanted to get out, I could've joined the army, you know. I did not use Irene." The last statement was more to himself. Like he needed to hear it out loud.

"So, where did you meet your wife?" I quickly resumed. "She was American, right?"

"Yes, Irene was from Connecticut. She was working in Glasgow for the summer, at a travel agency."

"And you went there to book a trip? To get out of Castlemilk?"

He grinned. I was finally getting the hang of it.

"And where were you planning on going?"

"To Florida, initially." He smiled absently. "It was going to be my first trip ever. Kinda like you getting out of Ontario. Let me tell you, I was nervous just entering that store. I'd just gotten off work and was all grungy and dirty. I thought they'd kick me out for sure. I must have looked like I couldn't afford it, anyway. But there she was. And she was kind, really took her time with me. And not long after that, we started going out. In the end, we went to Connecticut together. And I still haven't been to Florida."

Meeting Jillian in pretty much the same way he had met his wife must have felt like a déjà vu for him.

"So…did you really think Jillian would never find out you'd lied about your mother?"

I could tell my question surprised him. It took him a few seconds to respond.

"Well, I guess I knew it would happen sooner or later. I was going to tell her, eventually. But I never found the right time." Yeah, I knew exactly what he meant. Brett and I would have, eventually, split up. Sooner or later. At that right time that somehow never came.

"And then that lady came and aired all your laundry. Do you blame her?"

95

"Mrs. Wellish? You bet I do! She shoulda kept her big trap shut and—"

"No, not her. Do you blame Jillian?"

He seriously seemed to consider this for a moment. "Well, I'm not saying this was one of my most stellar moments, but—"

"But what? She was just overreacting in light of you practically ruining her? Her business, her credibility, her reputation?" Michael spit out those last few words, startling me. I hadn't noticed our time was up. "What do you think people will make of that, her dating her dead clients' husbands? You ruined her, you jerk! And you don't even see that? No wonder she's done with you!"

"Shut up, Michael." I gave him the evil eye. "This is my interview."

"Make sure to ask some of the hard questions, too. Like what was it like for your wife to feel like crap? To not have her husband there by her side? Was it because you weren't attracted to a bald woman? Or was that whole sickness part just too inconvenient for you? And—"

"Michael, that's enough." This time it was Jeremy who cut him off. "You'll get your chance to ask your questions later. Let Corinne finish up here. And then you can interview Trish."

"No, I wanna interview Stephen," he insisted through gritted teeth.

"We'll get to that. But for now, you'll interview Trish."

I had never heard Jeremy be that firm. It surprised me, and even Michael reluctantly backed off. He would have to question Stephen another time. Jeremy would reserve that interview for the very end. That first day, it was just me and Stephen, Michael and Trish. But we were finally getting some footage. Or so I thought.

* * * *

Trish Grady

I was scared of Michael. Why did I have to start with him? I wished I could have faced one of the others first. Just to give me some time to ease into these interviews.

I decided to let Michael go first to cater to what Corinne called his "control freak nature." His questions were cold and calculated. From the get-go it was obvious he was going to portray me in a certain, unflattering light. He wouldn't ask about my kids, the impact of their father being in jail, or my harrowing ordeal having to turn my own husband in. No, nothing that could garner me compassion from the audience or the producers. Instead, he kept asking me about *Crystal Falls*. Whether I had seen every episode. He inquired about my favorite story lines and characters. After all, I was a housewife with nothing else to do but to sit on my big fat butt and watch TV all day.

When I finally did try to talk about that fateful November night—the one that practically destroyed my whole family—he quickly dismissed it as "the unfortunate accident." Can you believe it? That's definitely not what it was to me. When I hit the brakes that night, life as I knew it came to screeching halt.

I was angry, but too scared to let it show. And when my turn came to interview Michael, I honestly didn't know what to ask him. The one question on everyone's mind was whether he had killed his wife. But I was not going to open that can of worms. Let Stephen deal with that (he, no doubt, would). I decided to play sympathetic.

"Looking back, you've certainly gone through a lot the last few years. The loss of your wife, having to close down your business, the trial…" It wasn't even a question, but it was enough to get him started.

He nodded. "It was certainly more than I'd ever thought I'd face in this lifetime. But it was also a time I learned to appreciate the support of my family and friends. People that believed in my innocence and stood by me." He sounded like a press release, and I felt even more disdain.

"But let's not forget, even before your wife's death, things weren't easy for you. I understand you lost your business." Again, more of a statement than an actual question. And honestly, motivated by my sheer contempt for the man. I couldn't resist.

"Yes," he said now in a grave voice, "that was like another death right there. Ten years down the drain. All the time and effort Julian and I put into that venture. And in the end, nothing to show for it. You have no idea what that is like." Yes I did, you jerk. Fourteen years of marriage. Fourteen years of building a family, being at everyone's beck and call. Fourteen years and nothing to show for it.

He dissected the reasons for his business failure with painstaking detail derived from some market analysis. Normally, I would have been plain bored. But in light of the far greater tragedy of his wife's death? How many more times did he have to lament those *ten years down the drain*? What about his seventeen-year marriage? So far it hadn't come up once. It was clear what had affected him the most. I just hoped the producers would arrive at that same conclusion. Maybe even the police would. If he'd killed once just for an insurance payout, he wouldn't think twice about murdering Rob. Or the other contestants who stood in the way of his money.

When we were finally done, I rushed upstairs to vent in my diary. But I couldn't find it anywhere in my desk. My rib cage constricted. First Michael's laptop and now this. I searched through my dresser, under my pillow, even in my night table drawers. Nothing. I felt nauseous. Somebody had been in my room. Maybe even at night while I'd slept! Someone had gone through my things. I felt violated. Some stranger now got to read all my thoughts and innermost feelings. And what if whoever stole it showed it to the producers? Would they try to use this against me somehow? I had said some not-so-nice things about Jeremy in there. I was kicking myself. I should never have written any of this down. The house just wasn't safe.

* * * *

Jeremy Lawren

I wasn't happy with our shooting tapes. I had been hoping for some juicier material. Maybe just to impress Detective Hail. Or maybe three years of working with Rob had rubbed off on me.

Nevertheless, I made my way to the police station the next morning. I had to show them I was doing my part. Not that I thought there was anything substantial on there. Little did I know, there was literally nothing on there.

The phone rang at the mansion later that afternoon.

"The tapes are blank, Jeremy," Detective Hail informed me. "Completely blank."

I must have looked perturbed. Corinne immediately put a hand on my arm. "Everything okay?"

"I… I'll be right over," I stammered into my phone and hung up. "Sorry, guys, just some problems on the set. Why don't you take the afternoon off? Maybe we can shoot some more tonight."

I looked like a complete idiot, I thought angrily on my way over to the station. I had blown it. Now they'd send in one of their undercover guys, for sure. 'Cause I was obviously too stupid to hit record. I had worked on a set for the past three years and couldn't find the button? Impossible. It had to be sabotage. Someone was bent on us not getting any footage.

"Maybe someone switched the tapes?" I suggested.

Hail looked at me, intrigued. "What was on there?"

Absolutely nothing of interest, I assured him. Discussions about low-income housing, Michael's failed business, and Trish's TV watching habits.

Hail nodded. "Is there any possibility you could have not hit record?"

On four separate occasions? I frowned. I definitely preferred the thought of sabotage.

"Well, for now don't tell the contestants the tapes are blank," he instructed me. "Let's pretend we don't have a clue. Just say the tapes are kept over at Skyview and will be looked at later. In the meantime, you continue shooting with them. We'll see what happens. If the next set of tapes turns out blank too, I'd say we're on to something."

I nodded. "One more thing. Michael insists someone stole his laptop from his room. And last night Trish came down complaining that someone took her diary. She said she always kept it inside her desk, but now it's gone."

Hail took note. "A laptop stolen. Interesting. Any idea what was on there?"

"According to Michael, just his thoughts and notes on our shoot at the mansion. He had written some sort of outline." I rolled my eyes. "He's crowned himself director, if you know what I mean."

Hail grinned. "And you think one of the others took it?"

"I really don't know. Wouldn't put it past Stephen. Just to bug him." I had kept Hail up-to-date about the ongoing feuds.

"It's possible," he agreed. "Both the laptop and the diary thefts could well be just a thing between competitors. They could be spying on each other. Trying to get in each other's head to see who might have an edge over them. But if someone is interfering with your shoot, I'd say we're dealing with something more serious."

"Why would anyone have an interest in us not filming the contestants?" I asked. "It's just a stupid little publicity thing."

Hail shrugged. I wondered how much he was telling me. Was he really letting me in on the investigation? Maybe he knew a lot more but chose to keep me in the dark.

"Did you find anything in Rob's notes?" I asked him straight out.

"No." He shook his head, and I couldn't help but feel he was being sincere. "We found nothing in his files but the entries your four finalists had mailed him. And you have read those yourself. I understand you picked them, right?"

Yes, and I had been kicking myself steadily since.

"At this time, we have to pursue all angles," Hail said. "And with that many people on set, you can imagine the amount of work involved. Interviewing everyone, verifying alibis... And we can't rule out any of your contestants either. Especially since Rob mentioned something didn't add up within their stories. But, again, we can't be sure he was serious. He might have just been trying to create some hype."

I sighed. "True. Wouldn't have been unlike Rob. But one thing I'm certain of is that I did hit record. I'm sure those tapes weren't blank."

"Like I said, just keep filming. And we'll see about that next batch."

* * * *

Stephen Dowell

Jeremy was gone, and we were stuck here with Trish yammering on and on about some missing diary. Come on, why would any of us have taken it? Well, Michael, maybe. Seemed like something he might do. Just to get back at Trish in case she stole his laptop. Weird, though; I thought he had concluded that was me.

Who keeps a diary, anyway?

* * * *

Michael Palmer

I'm not sure I believed her. Who would have an interest in Trish's diary? The woman talked non-stop; what more was there to say? I doubted she had any unexpressed thoughts left in her head. I vented my frustrations to Julian that night, as usual.

"She probably just made the whole thing up," he agreed. "After all, someone did take your laptop. Now she better show people are after her stuff as well."

"Stupid competition." I groaned.

He laughed softly. "What did you expect? You went on a reality show. Don't say I didn't warn you."

"Yeah, well, next time remind me to listen."

* * * *

Corinne Prichett

Ha, served her right! I could just picture what was in there. Page after page of her rambling on about us, why none of us deserved to win… And now someone got to read the whole thing. Funny! No wonder she was that worried! Whoever took it, I hoped they passed it on to the producers. Served her right.

* * * *

Jeremy Lawren

I made my way back to the mansion, dreading the full account of the quarrels that had, no doubt, taken place in my absence.

I started fabricating some lame story about an unspecified continuity problem to explain my sudden departure. My thoughts kept revolving around *Crystal Falls*, the show I had come to loathe more each season. The LA traffic bothered me more than usual, and thinking about my four taxing roommates didn't put me in any better mood. I was ready to move back to Georgia.

Then it hit me so abruptly I slammed the brakes, almost causing the guy behind me to rear-end my car. He honked his horn in disgust. The police said they found nothing in Rob's files but the contestants' initial entries. But that simply wasn't true. I had seen other papers. There was Trish's petition for divorce (ironically, filed by her husband, not her). And Stephen's marriage license. Irene had been previously married, something he had never brought up. Then there was the death certificate of Michael's father-in-law who had passed away shortly after Michael's arrest. I even remembered a newspaper article about a convenience store fire, the place where Corinne used to work. Initially they had suspected arson. But a small correctional notice later pointed to an electrical fire. At the time, none of those things seemed like the "bombshell" Rob had promised. But now… It was enough to make me turn back around.

* * * *

Trish Grady

You had to feel a bit sorry for Jeremy. The poor kid got it from all sides. *Crystal Falls* had run into some major continuity problems. After the fire had destroyed nearly all of their set, the crew had to shoot a lot of the footage outside. He had to step out for emergency meetings on several occasions. They were desperately trying to rework their story lines around those new locations. Believe me, that would never have happened under Rob.

On top of that, the producers were all over Jeremy for his lack of initiative on our shoot here at the mansion. While they liked the idea of the contestants interviewing one another, they insisted he take a more active role and participate. And, as he informed us with a pained smile, unfortunately that meant the questions were going to get a bit tougher. I wondered if someone was finally going to step up and ask Michael whether he had killed his wife.

"So what did the producers not like about the footage we got so far?" Michael wanted to know. He was probably miffed they didn't like his directing.

"To be honest, I don't think they've gone over the tapes yet," Jeremy admitted. I was disappointed. I was hoping for some feedback. "They got their hands full with *Crystal Falls* right now, as you can well imagine. They probably won't get to it for a while."

"So how do they know it's all crap then?" Stephen clearly did not relish the idea of having to start over. "Granted, it is all crap, but—"

"Look, nobody said you guys did a bad job." Jeremy raised his hands, fending off the oncoming wave of criticism. "The producers were just a bit concerned that, well, if you guys interview one another, the portrayals wouldn't be all that objective. They still like the idea, but they want me to participate as well. Kinda like an umpire. 'Cause if I completely leave the interviews to you, it could be...a bit slanted."

"Ha, that's what I said!" I blurted out, garnering me disdainful looks from both Corinne and Michael. But it's true, I did say that.

* * * *

And so we started over the next day. I got to go first and, this time, picked Stephen. Simply because he was the least likely to have taken my diary. Of course the things I'd written down there weren't all that flattering. But it was never meant for anyone else to read, right? I don't know why I didn't believe Stephen took it. I guess he just didn't seem the least bit interested in me or my thoughts. Actually, I couldn't picture him reading much of anything. He groaned now, mainly because he hated getting up early in the morning. I guess he was used to working nights.

"So, you never watched *Crystal Falls*," I started, a little uncertain. I honestly didn't know what to ask the guy. I mean, this was supposed to be all about *Crystal Falls*, and he clearly hated the show. Though, how could he if he hadn't seen a single episode?

"My wife, ehm… my late wife used to watch it all the time," he said, insinuating that her viewing habits were enough for the both of them.

"And you never once joined her?" Jeremy asked. "Just to keep her company? Even when she got sick?"

"It's on during the day. That's when I sleep. Remember, I work nights?" Stephen grumbled.

"And when your wife got sick, you continued working? You didn't cut back on your hours?" I asked, in line with the newer, tougher questions.

"Irene didn't want me to."

"Of course she would've wanted you to!" I argued. "How could she not? You were her husband! That means in sickness and in health. Remember that part?" That's what marriage was for, to care for each other, right? I wondered. If I had gotten sick, would that have changed anything in my marriage? No, Bill probably wouldn't have taken care of me either. Of course he wouldn't have. He left a kid to die. So why would he have cared about me?

"Irene wanted things to go on as usual. That's what she always said," Stephen insisted, and I could feel the blood boiling in my veins.

"And you believed her?" My voice came out shrill, which probably didn't make for a very good interview. Pardon me, I have no patience for murderers, liars, and selfish jerks. Of course the poor woman had told him not to bother. She probably felt guilty having gotten sick in the first place. And he, conveniently, went along with it. He wouldn't bother. I suddenly felt anguish for this stranger who had spent the last few months of her life so alone.

"Look," Stephen said, his voice hard, "you wanna know the truth? I don't think she would have wanted to have me around, okay? I would've been useless, completely useless. There was nothing—you hear me, nothing!—I could do for her."

Jeremy looked at his feet. He clearly wasn't cut out for these tougher new interviews. But I wasn't willing to let Stephen off quite so easily.

"Nobody wants to be alone," I pointed out. I knew that from experience. In online surveys I still wouldn't check the "divorced" box. "I'm sure she would have wanted you there. Nobody wants to go through something like that alone."

"You think leaving her behind felt good?" Stephen scoffed back at me. "Every time I left for my shift, I kept thinking, 'This might be the last time...' And every time I got back in, she'd be there on the couch. And I'd go up to her, carefully, 'cause she might be asleep. I wouldn't want to wake her 'cause she was always in pain. I'd go up there, carefully, carefully, checking... checking if she was still breathing. That's all I could think of, every time I looked at her. Is she still alive?" His voice broke, that last part was barely audible. He bit his lip, trying hard to maintain his composure. He certainly wouldn't want to cry in front of me, the stupid housewife who spent her days watching *Crystal Falls*.

For the first time I honestly wondered what we were doing here. Was it really worth it? Was it worth going through all those painful memories just so some TV viewers could pass an otherwise uneventful afternoon?

"That's all I could think of," Stephen repeated now, more to himself than to anyone in the room. "I'm gonna be alone soon. Believe me, she did not want to be around me like that. You think I was good company?"

No, and neither was I. Every time I looked at Bill, I knew I was going to be alone soon. The day would come—the woman would come—that final fling that would drive that last nail in the coffin of our marriage. My kids would leave home. I'd be alone. I always knew.

"Maybe it really was easier for her without you around," I admitted slowly. "It probably made it harder for her, seeing you in that much pain."

* * * *

Stephen Dowell

That, quite honestly, was the most insightful thing that had come out of her mouth so far. I think Irene did not want me to be there when she went. She passed away one night shortly after I'd started my shift. I got the call I had been dreading for months. I made my way back to the hospital, where she had spent the last two nights. It was finally over.

Yet it somehow wouldn't sink in that she was gone. No matter how much I had rehearsed that moment in my mind, it seemed surreal. It was like someone had hit me in the gut. I felt nauseous for weeks.

I went back to work shortly after. I had to. My dad did the same thing after my mother died, and I finally understood why. Somebody once told me even the disciples did it, right after Jesus was crucified. They went back fishing. It was the only thing they remembered to do.

It's a good thing I worked the nightshift, you know. The nights at home would have driven me up the wall. I would have started drinking, for sure. But I'm not an alcoholic, believe me. I know better. That's the one thing Castlemilk taught me. You learn not to fall into that trap. 'Cause once you're an alcoholic, you never get out. And like Corinne said, you gotta get out. She was a lot smarter than they gave her credit for. She'd read a lot, you could tell. People thought she was stupid, keeping that ring, bragging about the fantasy boyfriend. Just goes to show, don't try to be something you're not. Hadn't worked out for me either.

And now I sat there, opposite Trish, and I really didn't have any questions. Yeah, it sucked her husband had cheated on her. It sucked for the kids that their dad was in jail (which, by the way, in Castlemilk would've gone largely unnoticed). But this was Cicero, she assured me, and they simply couldn't stay after that. Hence, they moved in with her parents. Poor Jeremy and I sat through a ten-minute rant about insensitive remarks, her mother's overly picky house rules, and nosy neighbors dropping by. I still didn't care.

That's one thing about Irene, she always cared about people. Maybe my care died with Irene, who knows. But I did care about

Jillian. No, I cared about what Jillian thought of me. That's not the same as caring. So maybe I really didn't care. I didn't care when that Rob guy turned up dead, and that's pretty sick. Maybe I'm a psychopath. Maybe my alter ego even took Michael's stupid laptop. Yeah, I could've done it, just to mess with him. So don't put it past me just yet.

* * * *

Jeremy Lawren

If I hadn't been bent on proving I wasn't too dumb to hit record, I would have given up right there. Stephen was a million miles away. And I failed to see how the husband being in jail impacted the sale of Trish's house. I kept my eye on the tiny red LCD burning bright, indicating this was definitely going to tape. Stephen yawned heartily.

"What were you expecting?" he said, and I remember being genuinely surprised that he actually had followed the conversation. "They are his family. Of course they're gonna blame you!"

"So you think men have the right to have affairs once they tire of their wives?" Trish's eyes flashed with anger. At that moment, Stephen probably embodied every scumbag husband on earth.

"That's not what I said. Jeremy, help me out here!" he pleaded.

"You were an easy target," I offered.

She fixed two hostile eyes on me now. "And why is that—because I was a fat, ugly housewife, and no wonder he was cheating on me?"

"Nice one." Stephen grinned in my direction.

I heaved a sigh. "That's not what I meant." There was clearly no good way out of that one. "Look, your husband is a jerk. Nobody's debating that. He left a guy for dead. I mean, what was his mother supposed to do with that? Of course she'd blame you. He was speeding because he was being followed. He cheated because he was unsatisfied in his marriage. Excuses, excuses, blah, blah, blah. But you can't expect anything else from her. After all, she's his mother. You'd do the same thing for your kids. You'd stick up for them, right?" That last statement seemed to appeal to the parent in her. For a moment the wrinkles on her forehead softened ever so slightly.

"That woman systematically tried to annihilate my reputation," Trish resumed, back in her old frenzy. "Like the entire thing was my fault."

"Nobody thinks that," I assured her, despite the fact that several people, including Rob, had believed exactly that. And Rob had turned up dead.

* * * *

112

Corinne Prichett

"Have you found your laptop?" I don't know why I started with that one. 'Cause even if Michael had found it, he wasn't likely to admit it.

"No," he said curtly, taking a slow sip from his water glass.

"And which one of us do you suspect took it?" I asked.

He glared at me and shrugged. "Frankly, it could have been any one of you."

"And tell me, exactly why would we do such a thing?"

He sneered. "None of you have been very cooperative throughout this shoot, for whatever reasons. Let's just leave it at that."

"And you're okay being filmed?" Jeremy asked from behind the camera.

"Me? Sure." Michael nodded, seemingly surprised he had to ask. "I have nothing to hide. I stand by every word of my story. I always have. I'm not afraid of the publicity."

"You think we made our stories up?" I asked, more than a little irritated. Trish was right. He was doing his best to discredit us at any given opportunity.

"Who knows," he replied, again cradling the water glass in his hand. "Look, all I'm saying is that if you're that certain your story is true, well… then you got nothing to hide. And we should be done here in no time."

"Did your family believe in your innocence?" I asked him point blank, focusing the interview back on him.

"Of course they did," he replied, visibly annoyed. Good. Looked like I finally got to him.

"What about your wife's family?" Jeremy chimed in.

"They all know I'm innocent. Anyone who has known me for any length of time knows I could never have done something like that." Now that, technically, wasn't true. Stephen, Trish, and I had known him for a few weeks, and none of us were so sure. "I loved my wife. It's true. In spite of all the difficulties we had—and I've always admitted we had some difficulties—I loved my wife. I am not a cold-blooded murderer. We were married for seventeen years. I cared deeply for her."

"But you do understand it looks like you had a motive?" I couldn't resist pointing out.

"Nonsense." He put the glass down with an angry thud. "Things were already turning around. I had gotten a new job that day. And my father-in-law was now receiving adequate care. We were finally getting back on track."

"How did your father-in-law take the news?" Jeremy wanted to know.

"I... I don't think he actually comprehended what happened," Michael conceded. "By that time he didn't recognize any of us anymore. He didn't even remember he had a daughter."

"But you did tell him?" I asked curiously. I wouldn't have put it past him not to tell the old man.

"Julian did." He looked straight at me, his hands neatly folded on his lap. They were steady, I noticed. But liars don't fidget, contrary to what people believe. They need to focus all their energy on getting their stories straight.

"Look, my father-in-law wasn't doing well at that point. He died shortly after. His health had been failing for a long time. And on top of that, he had contracted a virus that was making the rounds in the nursing home. I think three or four people died that month."

I once read that people who lied paused longer. But he didn't do that. His speech was eloquent, almost too well rehearsed. Maybe he had been over these questions too many times. I decided to go for something unexpected.

"Which one of us do you like the least?" I blurted out.

"What?" It worked. He seemed genuinely surprised.

"You heard me. Which one of us do you like the least?"

His shoulders slouched. Now he just seemed tired and worn out, much like the rest of us. It made him a little more human. "Look, it's not that I have anything against you guys. I think some of you have made some bad choices, but..."

"But?" I asked curiously.

"But you would probably say the same about me, right?"

Right. I would have closed down the company, and a lot sooner. I would have divorced Karen if she had made it clear that's what she wanted. Why waste your time with someone who doesn't want to be with you?

"It's not that easy," Michael said now. "I believe it's our responsibility to make things work."

"But at all costs?"

"Yes." He nodded. "At all costs."

* * * *

Jeremy Lawren

I have often wondered what it was about me that conveyed the idea that I was not very motivated. I considered myself quite ambitious. But others didn't see that. Rob never did. He'd assumed I would be the underpaid help for the rest of my life. That's precisely why he had hired me in the first place. I wasn't after his job. I was in that point five percent margin of people here in Hollywood who didn't want to direct. I was no threat. And at the moment, it was precisely what I was going for.

They never assumed I was watching them. Never assumed I'd found out about the tapes being blank. Never assumed I was doing anything but the bare minimum. Just here to crank out that stupid little reality shoot because the producers had asked me to.

The mood in the house had changed ever so slightly. They had moved from open hostility to quiet resignation. Not that they liked each other any more than before. But they had stopped the fighting. Maybe to conserve energy. They didn't want to waste their time and effort. Or maybe they had come to realize these ongoing feuds weren't endearing them to the producers. You know, the guys who would eventually crown one of them the winner.

I had popped two days' worth of interview tapes in my trunk when I realized my laptop was still in my bedroom. I went back inside to retrieve it. With Michael's already missing, I didn't want to risk another theft.

My window ajar, I could hear them on the patio below. I was surprised they hung out together. Maybe bad company was better than no company at all. Only Corinne wasn't with them, I noted.

"Where's Jeremy off to?" Trish wanted to know.

"I dunno. But give the guy a break. He's allowed a night off." Thank you, Stephen.

"Maybe we should go out too," Trish suggested. "Beats hanging around here every night."

"I like it here," Michael said sarcastically. "I'm in Hollywood. Now if that's not a dream come true…"

"You guys are such an ungrateful bunch." Trish again. "I, for one, will go down to the set again tomorrow to watch some more of the filming. Jeremy said they're back up and running. And I still like *Crystal Falls*. I'm not gonna let any of you guys spoil it for me."

"Here, let me spoil it for you," Michael offered. "Ivy's gonna set fire to the whole fashion empire. Arson—probably brought on by someone dumb enough to light up another prop. End of show. Grand series finale." That was, indeed, more plot than we'd seen the last three years. And it would get me back to Georgia. I was quite willing to go with that.

"None of you deserves to win." Trish sounded angry. "If you don't like the show, you should just get out."

"Believe me, that has crossed my mind."

"More than once," Stephen added solemnly.

"Who cares about the show; where else can you make two hundred grand?" Corinne suddenly chose to join them. "Don't pretend it's anything else. I'm sure even Jeremy only stays on for the money."

She should see my paycheck. Couldn't be the money. What on earth was I doing here then? Right, it was only temporary. Just until I found my true calling.

"Why do you think they suddenly added this reality shoot about us?" Michael asked, still suspicious.

"Cheap publicity," Corinne unceremoniously summed it up.

"Maybe they want to show how we interact. A study of human nature and how we change over time, living here under one roof," Trish pondered. "Just like any other reality show, I guess."

"People don't change," Stephen scoffed. "It's true. I'm exactly the same person I was when I was eighteen. All that stuff about age making you wiser—total baloney!"

"In your case I believe that to be true," Michael said acidly.

"You don't think I'll be any different in my thirties?" Corinne wondered.

"Look, I took soccer too seriously when I was eighteen. And guess what, I still do! It's not something you magically outgrow. The only difference is now I know I take it too seriously. So big whoop. Don't change a thing."

I could practically hear Michael rolling his eyes. "Is there any iced tea left?" he said now, obviously done listening to Stephen's take on life.

"I think so. Check the fridge."

"Anybody else want something from the kitchen?"

"I'll come with you," Trish announced. "I'm getting a little chilly. I better grab a sweater."

Chairs were moved. I could hear the patio doors slide. Then a few moments of awkward silence.

"I found it," Stephen said in a hushed tone.

"Found what?" Corinne asked.

"Michael's laptop."

"You found Michael's laptop? Where?"

"Downstairs. It's in the weights room."

"Why didn't you tell him?" Corinne immediately wanted to know.

"Tell him? No way. That's just what he wants, me finding it. 'Cause then he can say I did it. That's why he put it in the weights room, for sure. He knows that neither you nor Trish ever go down there. No way I'm gonna touch that thing and get my fingerprints on it."

"You think he hid it himself?"

"Well, I sure didn't, and neither did you. And I doubt Trish took it. So that leaves only him."

"Or Jeremy."

"Nah. Jeremy is a nice kid." Thanks again, Stephen. But why would Michael hide his own laptop? It didn't make any sense. Hide it just to point fingers at Stephen?

"Michael really is a jerk. He constantly tries to make us look bad... like our stories are just a bunch of hype. When his is the only one never fully proven. For all we know, he could've killed his wife. There could be a murderer in the house!"

"You know what," Stephen said a little hesitantly. "I actually don't think he did it. I used to think so. But not anymore."

"You got any proof?" Corinne asked, more than a little surprised.

"Look, I don't like the guy any more than you do. And for a while I wanted to believe he did it, but then...I just don't think it adds up. Just think about it, when he—"

"Shhh... they're coming back."

The patio doors whooshed open once again. Michael came back out, followed shortly after by Trish. Stephen eventually disappeared inside (presumably to go to the washroom). And I hovered behind my bedroom shutters for anther fifteen minutes without getting to hear why Michael hadn't killed his wife.

* * * *

It was going on ten when I finally snuck out of the house. My car, a rusty blue '94 Escord, was parked around the corner. I had bought it from a used car dealer who, less than a month later, made the top ten of the city's worst. "Jeremy only stayed for the money." Yeah, right. The trunk squeaked rhythmically as I drove down the street. It hadn't closed properly in months. Occasionally it popped open in mid-ride, as it did that very moment, forcing me to pull over. I got out, angry at that piece of junk. Angry I was still stuck in LA. Angry at Corinne for, once again, assuming I wasn't a hard worker. Only here for the money. Had a look at my crap car lately?

I was about to slam the trunk when I saw it. The tapes were gone. The trunk was empty.

* * * *

"I know what you're thinking," I told Hail right after I broke the news that there, again, were no tapes. "I put them in the trunk, for sure. Someone must have taken them. The trunk doesn't close properly. It hasn't in a while."

Hail studied me, no doubt wondering why I had even put them in the trunk knowing full well it was unsafe storage. Stupid. But I only went back to the house to grab my laptop. I never meant to hang around that long.

"And in that time, who had access to your car?" Hail wanted to know.

Corinne hadn't been with them at the start, it occurred to me. And Trish went back inside with Michael, allegedly to grab a sweater. Though it wasn't all that cold tonight. Actually, each one of them had, at some point, gone inside the house and returned a short while after. The car was parked right around the corner. Whoever wanted those tapes would have had enough time to grab them out of the trunk. Which meant whoever took the tapes must have realized I was still in the house.

119

"Maybe it's time to beef up security," Hail mused out loud.

"Look, it won't happen again," I assured him, still embarrassed. "Next time I won't leave the tapes out of my sight."

"I mean your security," he said curtly, and it sent chills down my spine. "I think we should send someone in with you. One of us could pose as a camera op. I don't want to put you in any danger."

"I don't think I am," I lied. As scary as living with a potential murderer was, I was not ready to hand this over. "Look, if you send someone in now, the contestants will only get suspicious. I'll mention I was about to drop the tapes off at Skyview, but must have misplaced them somewhere. I'll suggest they help me look. It's better to let whoever is sabotaging the shoot think I'm too stupid to notice."

Hail rubbed his chin. "Fine. But listen... if anything more happens, that's it. Then I can no longer guarantee for your safety. At that point we'll have to step in."

I nodded. All I needed was one more shot.

* * * *

Trish Grady

I wondered what she was up to now. You couldn't trust her. Either Corinne and Stephen had become a couple, or she was simply using him to make Jeremy jealous. But the two of them were always together now. Always talking, then falling silent when anyone else came near. Maybe they were plotting to somehow eliminate Michael and me and split the prize. But I kept my eye on them. And so did Jeremy. I could tell he was studying them on a few occasions.

"You think there's something between those two?" I finally asked Michael, doing my best to sound casual.

"Corinne and Stephen?" Michael snickered. I was surprised he hadn't noticed. "Trish, you really watch too much TV."

I tried not to show I was offended. That was exactly what Bill used to say when he would brush me off. And even back then my instincts had proven right.

"I'm just saying they're awfully chummy, those two. And I don't trust her. She's a calculating little—"

"Who is?" Jeremy walked onto the patio that very moment.

"Trish is convinced Corinne and Stephen are a couple." It did sound silly, hearing it out of Michael's mouth.

"Ah, an on-set romance. Our own little soap. That would have been right up Rob's alley! Too bad he didn't live to see that," Jeremy said mockingly. I thought it was callous, in light of his boss's tragic end. What did we really know about Jeremy, anyway? So, he was at the police station that night. That could have been well timed. All he had to do was pay a hitman… But did he have that kind of money? Wait, the two hundred grand had gone missing… I wondered if the thought had crossed anyone's mind. I glanced at Michael, but he seemed oblivious.

"There's no way those two are a couple," Michael said now. "Like her or not, Corinne is not that ugly. She could do way better than Stephen. I think Trish here is just a little paranoid."

"I am not," was all I could say. Me paranoid? That was rich, coming from him. After all, I wasn't the one constantly checking in with my lawyer or ex-business partner and accusing others of stealing my belongings. I never accused anyone, you know.

121

Though I did believe Corinne took my diary. Who else would have?

"I'm curious now," Jeremy said, and I couldn't tell if he was serious. "Let's see what those two are talking about."

* * * *

Jeremy Lawren

"I still don't know why you would say that." Corinne leaned over, refilling Stephen's iced tea. Poor Trish, I could see why she was jumping to conclusions. Not that I thought those two actually were a couple. It could well have been a calculated effort. Anything to push Trish's buttons. Get her to have a meltdown, preferably on camera.

"All I'm saying is, it's just not like him," Stephen replied. "Look, I know his type. Money is not what makes guys like him tick. Money is part of it, sure. There's a certain prestige he likes to maintain—"

"But that's exactly it. He didn't have any money. His business went under. So there's his wife's life insurance and—"

"No," Stephen shook his head. "He's not stupid. He would have known the police would catch on to that. And then what? They'd be all over his financial affairs, the state of his marriage... For guys like him, that's a killer. You think he'd want to see that all over the papers? No way. He would've thrown himself off the balcony before he'd share his failures with everyone."

"He's quite willing to share everything on national TV now," Corinne pointed out, voicing my own thoughts.

"He's willing to share his side of the story. Big difference." Stephen took a long sip of iced tea. I was close enough to hear the clink from his glass. "And think about it; he really doesn't have much choice. The damage is already done. So now he's going on the offensive."

"I still don't know how you can be so sure. I'm not convinced he didn't do it."

"Well, look at his past behavior. He's the kind of guy who simply cannot admit defeat. His business was barely scraping by for years. The marriage was limping along. But he kept at it, trying to make it work. He couldn't let people see that he'd failed. He's always keeping the charade up."

"Yes, and he needed her life insurance money to do that. And that's why he killed her," Corinne concluded.

"No." Stephen shook his head again. "The timing was off, if you ask me. He had already started closing up shop when his wife died.

People already knew he had failed. Her death only made things worse for his reputation."

Corinne was quiet for a while. "But what if his wife had died the year before? Then what? Would you still believe in his innocence?"

Stephen didn't say anything. He didn't have to. We all knew the answer. Michael did seem capable of murder.

* * * *

"Hey guys." Jeremy appeared beside us. How long had he been standing there?

"Do we have to do more interviews today?" I asked, hoping my face hadn't turned beet red.

"Tonight maybe," he replied. "I was going to ask if you would like to go back to the set. You could catch a bit more of the shoot. I know you didn't get to see much so far. But I think they're all finished with the repairs."

The fire. I had almost forgotten about it. And before that, the set had been closed for the police investigation. I wondered if there were any further leads in Rob's death by now.

"So, you guys wanna come?" Jeremy repeated his invitation. I didn't, but in light of the two hundred grand was still willing to feign interest in the show. So I slowly got up.

"Oh, I didn't mean right away." Jeremy smiled apologetically. "I was going to squeeze in a quick workout. Anyone want to join me?"

"I'll come with you," I said. I had never visited the weights room downstairs. But I was curious to see if Michael's laptop was still there.

"Stephen?"

"I'll pass." He leaned back in his lawn chair. There was no way he'd be found anywhere near that thing, I knew.

"I'll check for you if your cell phone is still down there," I offered.

"What?"

"Your cell phone. You said the weights room was the last place you saw it, right?" It took him a few seconds to comprehend what I was talking about.

"Right." He finally caught on. "I put it on that little bench, right next to the treadmill. But that was a couple of days ago. Who knows if it's still there?"

* * * *

It was. Michael's laptop was lying right there on the bench.

"Oh, look at that," Corinne, officially still searching for the cell phone, pretended to be surprised. "Isn't that Michael's?"

"Looks like it," I said, trying to sound equally casual.

"Should we tell him?" Corinne asked.

"Hang on." I grinned. "Let's check what's on there first. I'm curious now." I turned it on while Corinne kept a watchful eye on the stairs.

I gasped. "That's unbelievable."

"What? What's on there?" Corinne asked breathlessly.

"It doesn't boot up. Systems error. Start-up disk unreadable."

"What?" She stared at me wide-eyed. "How can that be? You think someone tampered with it?"

I had no idea. But at that moment we heard footsteps, so I quickly shut the laptop down. Corinne walked around the room, still pretending to look for that cell phone. She made her way around the pool. She carefully checked the towel closet, and even behind the lawn chair covers.

"What's in here?" She walked to the end of the room, then unsuccessfully turned the handle of the door beside one of the basement windows. "It's locked."

I shrugged. "I think that's the electrical room. The owner probably doesn't want strangers to mess with it."

"What if we have a power outage and need to get to the switchbox?" she wanted to know.

"Then we'll have to break it open, I guess."

"Break what open?" Michael said from the stairs.

"The door to the electrical room."

"What for?"

"Nothing. We were just speaking hypothetically. You haven't seen Stephen's cell phone, have you?" I don't know why I asked. I was reasonably sure Stephen had never lost it.

"Nope. Say, is that my laptop?" He quickened his steps and picked it up from the bench. I held my breath.

"What is it doing down here? Did you guys take it?"

"Us? No, we didn't touch it." That, technically, wasn't true. But there was no way I was going to tell him I had tried to check on his files.

"What on earth…" He, no doubt, had just made the very same discovery I wasn't willing to admit to: the drive had been tampered with.

"Which one of you destroyed my disk?" He was furious now.

"It wasn't us," Corinne backed me up. "We were just down here looking for Stephen's cell phone."

"Stephen. Of course it was him!" Michael stormed off. I wondered if he was right.

* * * *

Michael Palmer

Yes, I was upset. That jerk had some nerve, wrecking my disk. The thought of him going into my bedroom, going through my personal belongings… He had violated my privacy. It was vandalism. This was…breaking and entering, at least!

Of course the coward denied it, as expected. I was furious. I would have loved to punch him out, but had enough sense to realize that, between the two of us, he probably had more bar fighting experience.

Jeremy watched our shouting match helplessly for a while, pleading with everyone to calm down. After all, they were expecting us over at the *Crystal Falls* set.

* * * *

Maybe, a long time ago, visiting a television studio would have sounded cool. Now it was just another tedious day spent in the company of people I had long started to loathe. I had debated staying behind, but Julian talked me out of it.

"I don't think that's a smart thing to do," he cautioned me. "Not with all the others going. You'll seem disinterested in the show." I definitely couldn't afford that. But not even Trish's over-the-top excitement seemed real anymore.

At first I wasn't sure how welcome we really were. When we walked in, Garth turned around, a bewildered look in his eyes. It took me a while to realize that Garth always had that look. It probably resulted from being shoved in charge of a TV production, something he didn't seem to know the first thing about. Granted, neither did I. But his repeated "Now could everyone listen to me for just a sec!" did nothing to establish him as the director. And I say this without the faintest hint of jealousy. Trust me, I wouldn't have wanted to be in charge of this nonsense either. I was astonished this crap actually made it on TV.

After a while I wandered off to explore the premises. Nobody seemed to care, anyway. And if anyone asked, I could always pretend to be looking for the washrooms. The place was quite a bit smaller than expected. Its narrow hallways made it look like any office building. Only signs like "Dressing Room 5" reminded we were in a TV studio. I turned when I heard steps behind me and was surprised to see Trish had followed me. Of all people, I would have expected her to stay glued to the set.

"It's kinda plain," she said, sounding a bit disappointed. "The building, I mean." I nodded, awkwardly noting we were alone in this hallway. Did it make her nervous to be here? Alone with the guy who maybe/possibly/surely killed his wife?

"You think this is where it happened?" She pulled me out of my thoughts, almost reverently pointing to the door labeled "Utilities 3".

"What?"

"You think this is where they found Rob?" she asked.

"I… I dunno. It's possible, I guess."

She briskly walked toward the door, which was not locked. She flicked the lights on. For a few moments we silently stared at shelves full of cleaning supplies, vacuum bags, and giant bottles of liquid soap. It seemed absurd, the two of us glued to this closet with a national TV production happening right next door.

"It's creepy," Trish whispered. Did she mean the closet or being alone with me? "Don't you think it's creepy to think that could be the murder weapon," she said now, pointing at the fire extinguisher.

"I doubt it's the one," I objected. "The police would have kept it. They would have sent it to the lab for fingerprints." I sounded like a guy with way too much experience.

"Quick, somebody's coming." She grabbed my arm and pulled me into the closet, swiftly hitting the light switch with the back of her hand. I simply cannot tell you what I felt at that moment. She believed me. This woman, standing less than six inches away from me in a dark utility closet, believed I hadn't killed my wife.

* * * *

Stephen Dowell

If there was a low point to this whole miserable experience, it was Michael accusing me of breaking and entering into his room. Well that, and the wasted hours spent on the film set.

All I could do was think about her. Irene, you won't believe this. This show was worse than I ever thought! The leading lady, Ivy, was bickering with her on-screen love interest, a guy at least twenty years her senior. He insisted he could only get ready in Dressing Room 3, which mistakenly had been assigned to her. Dressing Room 3 contained his favorite hair dryer, which, unfortunately, had been secured to the wall. Apparently hair dryers had a history of disappearing on the set. Maybe the actors weren't paid what we thought. Anyway, guys should not be allowed to have a favorite hair dryer, period. And guys with obvious hair pieces shouldn't pretend to need one.

"How long do we have to play fans here?" Corinne whispered beside me.

"That depends. What's your hourly wage?"

"Mine? I'm back down to about ten bucks."

"Let's see. Two hundred grand divided by ten. That's 20,000. You owe them 20,000 hours."

"Very funny—and depressing! I have to work 20,000 hours for what some actors make in a single episode!"

"Not these guys. Remember they're worried about their hair dryers!" I fished through my pockets and lit up a cigarette. Times like these called for desperate measures.

"You can't smoke in here!" Garth took two hectic steps toward me, hitting his knee on the prop side table. That must have hurt. But he always had that pained expression so you couldn't really tell.

"He panics now when he sees smoke on the set." Jeremy grinned from ear to ear. "Can't blame him."

"Fine, I'll take it outside."

"I'll come with you." Corinne jumped on the opportunity to head outside. I instinctively looked for Trish, who would see this as definitive proof we were a couple, and was surprised she wasn't there. And neither was Michael. Corinne and I were apparently the only die-hard fans watching the shoot! We should be allowed to split the prize between us just for that. Then they could use both our stories. Do what you want, make us a couple on the show. I didn't care anymore.

"You think Michael wrecked his disk just to set you up?" It seemed like way too much trouble to go through. Even for Michael.

"Who knows." Stephen blew a perfect smoke ring. I wondered how he did that.

"You'll have to give him that interview tonight," I pointed out.

"Yeah, don't remind me," Stephen said, pulling a face.

"Are you gonna ask him if he killed his wife?"

"What's the point?" He shrugged. "If he did kill her, he's not gonna admit to it. And if he didn't, well... people are still not gonna believe him."

"But... you said you believed him?"

"Yes."

"I still don't see what makes you so sure."

"Let's just say I know the type." He was quiet for a while, and I wondered what he meant. What type? The type who killed their wives?

"Irene was married to a guy like that," he said now, taking in a slow drag. "A total control freak. The type that simply cannot admit defeat. The marriage was over, but the guy refused to let go. That's why she came to Scotland for a while." He smiled sadly, absently playing with the lighter in his hand. I wondered how Garth would take us burning down the parking lot. The idea was tempting.

"Michael's just like that," Stephen concluded. "For him to close down his business... the whole world knew his shop had gone belly-up. Believe me, if he wanted to kill his wife, he would've done it long before."

"But she was going to file for divorce," I pointed out. "Maybe he tried to finish her off before the world knew his business and his marriage were over."

"Maybe, but not likely. Remember, their friends already knew. He said his wife had told several of them. No, when Karen fell over that balcony, it cost him one more thing: his reputation. He was the biggest loser in this."

"Maybe we all are," I said quietly. We had all lost something, and the only guy about to profit from our stories had turned up dead. We were both silent for a while.

"You know what's the worst?" Stephen looked at me, and I was taken aback by the intense sadness in his eyes. There was something permanent about it. Not the kind that could be washed out with a cry.

"I did all this for Irene. But that whole show, it's so... so beneath her. She was way too good for it. Even if they use her story—or mine—it wouldn't come close to who she was. That whole contest, I... I really don't care anymore." He sighed, forcing out an angry cloud of smoke. "But I'm starting to think that's what's wrong with me. I just don't care."

* * * *

Trish Grady

Maybe *Crystal Falls* died for me with Rob. Maybe I had changed. When Bill's infidelity was the worst thing in my life, I could escape to the show. I could relate to the heartaches of my favorite characters. But now that was gone, and I knew it. When the drama in your own life surpasses that on TV, it loses its appeal. And I guess it works the other way round, too. Miserable actors whose personal lives didn't match the excitement of their scripts. I had had my behind-the-scenes-look. For me the illusion was gone. Now it was just about the money.

Funny to think Corinne had been right all this time. I almost admired her for that. She'd seen through it so easily when I, fifteen years her senior, hadn't. One more thing to feel stupid about.

The ride back to the mansion was grotesquely quiet. We finally had one thing in common. None of us were fans of the show. I would have felt bad for Jeremy, but had the distinct feeling he was one of us. Us. Who were we, anyway? Maybe just a bunch of disgruntled folks that felt they'd gotten a raw deal. I wanted this whole stupid contest to be over. I looked at Stephen, dozing against the limousine window, and suddenly felt just as tired.

"One more round of interviews." Jeremy yawned. Right, I was supposed to talk to Corinne tonight.

* * * *

134

Jeremy Lawren

"Okay, folks, where is it?" I stared at my usual suspects lounging around the living room, looking for any telltale sign somebody knew what I was talking about.

"Is what?" Michael asked coolly.

"The camera. Very funny. Now where is it?" I repeated.

"The camera is gone?" Trish asked, a convincingly surprised look in her eyes. "It's rather large; how can it be gone?"

"That's exactly my question," I said, trying to stay calm. "And I'm hoping one of you can help me out here."

"You don't seriously believe one of us took the camera." Corinne pouted.

Stephen just looked at me and shook his head. I was too tired to argue.

"Maybe one of the cleaners moved it," Michael suggested, and for one moment, it seemed like a simple enough explanation. But nothing had been simple lately. I should've known better.

"Let's just have a look for it. There's no need to panic." Trish got up and made her way to the sun room. The others reluctantly dispersed.

My hand clenched into a fist. This was the last thing I wanted to be dealing with right now. Another sabotage. This was it. The cops would take over now. Did the others really believe I was that stupid? Hide the camera, Jeremy will never find it, shoot over? I was frustrated with myself. After all this time I still couldn't figure out which one of them was not telling the truth. Even Rob, the superficial showman, the guy who didn't give a crap about people, had seen through them. Granted, it hadn't done him any good. He should have kept his big mouth shut. But if I didn't have more insight than him, I'd never make it as a journalist.

So which one of them was lying? Lately, I kept wondering about Corinne. Just because it was a possibility I hadn't yet explored. Maybe her story had some holes. Unlike Trish, she had been standoffish toward Rob from the beginning. She never wanted to be alone with him. Though maybe that was just a sign of her common sense! But could she have driven out that night to deliver the fatal blow? I found it hard to picture. That kind of brute force was something I would have attributed to Stephen, not a small girl like her. Unless they had worked together... But whoever had done it had tried to stab Rob first. Maybe he was still moving, refusing to die. And then she panicked and had to finish it off.

It might surprise you I never suspected Michael, the fairly obvious choice. I didn't see what he stood to gain from Rob's death. He had already been acquitted of murdering his wife so even if Rob had dug up new evidence, he couldn't be tried again. And if anything, right after Rob's murder, he appeared to be... well, I guess "displeased" would describe it best. He came here to clear his name. But being at the center of another police investigation would achieve the exact opposite for him.

Then I heard it. An almost blood-curling scream from Trish. She was down in the basement. We rushed to her from all directions. And there, at the bottom of the pool, was the camera.

Corinne Prichett

The first time I was really scared was when I saw the camera. I grabbed Stephen's arm. The camera looked so corpse-like, lying there at the bottom of the water. Though a corpse would have floated, as Stephen immediately pointed out. His words did nothing to calm me down.

But why freak out at a soaked piece of equipment, when we had a dead director in a utility closet not too long ago? What was wrong with me?

* * * *

Michael Palmer

Oh, come on, it was Stephen. How could it be anyone else? Of course it was him. The guy knew I'd be interviewing him that night. Come to think of it, he couldn't have looked any more guilty. Took him forever to get his butt in gear and help us search for the camera. What a coward.

* * * *

Stephen Dowell

Call me crazy, I think it was Trish. Of course part of me wants to think it was Michael. But unfortunately, I don't believe he did it. He was too bent on grilling me that night. I knew it was breaking his heart it wasn't gonna come to that.

Why Trish? I dunno. But since I don't believe it was Michael or Corinne—and I'm reasonably sure it wasn't me!— well, that left only Trish, right? And she was the first to see it. It wouldn't have occurred to me to search for the camera downstairs. I thought she'd gone off to check in the sun room, anyway. So what was she suddenly doing in the basement? And now she was pretending to be all upset about it. But I don't think anyone really bought it. Not even Michael. Though he was quick to point fingers at me.

* * * *

Trish Grady

Of course the producers didn't trust us anymore. Not after this. I don't even think they trusted Jeremy. They assigned us a professional operator who kept an eye on camera number three day and night. He was a lovely young man around Jeremy's age. A redhead who had recently moved here from North Dakota. Jamie was his name, and he obviously wasn't used to the LA sun. He had burned both his arms badly riding his friend's motorcycle without protection.

By now we were out of bedrooms, so he had to share with Jeremy. Jamie was a really nice guy. Much more pleasant than the rest of the *Crystal Falls* crew had been. He seemed to take a genuine interest in us. And he was a very attentive listener, especially considering his young age. For him, it wasn't just about our silly shoot. I had quite a few talks with him without the camera rolling. He enquired about Bill and the kids, how they were taking their father's absence, and what living with my parents again was like. In a quiet moment, he even asked me about the other contestants. But I was careful not to badmouth any of them. It's always ugly when people resort to that. And you see it all the time on reality TV. Of course then you hope that's the person who gets booted off next. Just to stop the fighting.

"Must be hard for you guys, all under one roof," Jamie noted. "After all, you're not here to make friends. I bet that was Rob's idea. He was big on drama. But you'll probably be pretty glad when this is over. Can't blame you."

"Yes and no," I lied. "We're competitors, that's true. But at the same time...well, we've all been through a lot. So I guess we have that in common."

"Yeah, I guess." He nodded, gently wiping over the lens of his camera. "But two hundred grand? Man, that would be nice."

"Yeah." I smiled, a bit sheepishly because I knew the crew members were paid rather poorly. Jeremy had let it slip a few times he wasn't making all that much. And I'd learned that Jamie had another part-time job. He did quite a few shifts at a downtown photo lab. The kid was working overtime for us.

"For most folks that's a lot of money," I said. "For instance, Corinne and Stephen are from some pretty poor backgrounds." The truth was, I myself had been hit pretty hard after the divorce. With my ex-husband in prison and the pending lawsuit from the accident victim... I didn't want to think about it. I didn't want my kids to grow up like Corinne or Stephen had. In dire circumstances, always aware there wasn't enough. Corinne got her back-to-school clothes from *Value Village*, desperately hoping nobody would recognize them as their old donation drop-offs. Stephen's family barely had enough money for food. He remembered his aunt making bread pudding for his twelfth birthday, which was right around the time his mother died. Not even that tragedy could tarnish the memory of bread pudding.

Jamie pulled me out of my thoughts. "What would you do with the money?"

I was quiet for a moment. I wanted to do so many things, at that particular moment I couldn't pin it down to one. "I'd try to rebuild my life somehow, I guess." Yes, that was exactly what I wanted to do. In some form or other, that's what we were all trying to do. Rebuild our lives.

* * * *

Jeremy Lawren

I wasn't thrilled when Hail moved in with us, for more than one reason. There was the obvious concern they could realize he was an undercover cop. I was particularly worried when he concocted that phony story about working part-time at a photo lab. Yeah, he had to explain his coming and going. But that stupid excuse was too dangerous. After all, Michael had a background in design and printing. What if he decided to involve him in a discussion?

Hail's presence also put an added strain on me. I was suddenly painfully aware that I was acting. Hail had turned into "Jamie." We had worked together for some time. This shoot would be our first big break.

And that's another thing that got to me: Hail had a decent job, while I still needed this break. But someone else was in charge now. They didn't trust me anymore. Maybe Michael was right, and we really do all want to direct.

Personally, I thought Hail focused too much on the money as the motive for Rob's murder. He went through great pains playing up his own financial troubles in an effort to get the four of them talking. It left a bad taste in my mouth, him pretending to be anything like them.

"I guess I could borrow the funds from my uncle," Hail said now. "I can pay him back over time. I could at least get the car stereo fixed. I hate to be stuck in traffic without it."

"Don't do it," Stephen cautioned. "Don't take anybody's handouts. It's just not worth it. My dad accepted a couch once from a guy he used to work for. And every time we saw him—or even worse, his wife—they kept bringing up THE COUCH. In church, at the store… how does THE COUCH look in your living room… how's THE COUCH holding up… sure glad you could use THE COUCH, blah, blah, blah. Trust me, you'll just end up feeling like some charity case. Not worth it."

"I'd say your whole car isn't worth it," I added. Where on earth had Hail found this lemon? Hey, maybe my Top Ten worst dealer was still in business! I guess he'd taken one look at my old junker and concluded this would make him blend in perfectly with the rest of the underpaid crew. An '87 Olds Cutlass. Yikes. That was bad, even for one of us.

We were down to the last couple of interviews. And so far, with nothing on tape but the introductory shoot. But I couldn't tell them that. Couldn't let on I knew. I hoped we weren't really obligated to put out a show. I hadn't dared to ask Garth about it. If we were, I'd be forced to use that tape we had filmed when Rob was still alive. It was the one thing the police had recovered over at Skyview. And it had taken them a while to figure out what it was. Rob had stuck it in an unmarked case and tucked it in a box labeled *"Crystal Falls"*. I wondered if the cops would let me use it. Granted, the tape was awful. But I had always assumed Rob would eventually reshoot the whole thing. Well, hopefully we'd get some usable footage today.

Trish would start with Corinne. Michael and Stephen retreated to their rooms. Maybe to give them some privacy. Maybe—in Michael's case—to first consult with his lawyer or at least with his buddy Julian. He'd be talking to Stephen later. I had mixed feelings about that. On the one hand it was the interview I was most apprehensive about. I might have to break up a fight should it turn physical. Yet it would also yield the best material. If only Rob was still alive for this!

"So, how would you describe the last few weeks?" Trish asked Corinne, and I considered my own answer to that question.

"It's been… tense, I guess, is the word. With Rob's murder and we still have no leads…" Corinne looked at me questioningly. "Is that okay, to bring up Rob's murder here? Or should we rather not talk about that on camera?"

"No, you can say whatever you like," Hail answered for me. "We can always edit it out later. Just be yourself."

What was Corinne really like as herself? What were any of them like when not forced to slug it out with a bunch of strangers on reality TV? At times, two hundred grand hardly seemed enough incentive to keep going.

"So, why is this contest so important to you?" Trish resumed.

Corinne thought for a moment. She truly had no other answer than the prize money. But would she say that on camera? And what would Hail make of that? It could instantly focus the investigation on her. I found myself fervently hoping she wasn't going to say that.

"'Cause I want things to change, I guess. You don't know what it's like to be broke." Corinne looked at Trish, followed by a moment of uncomfortable silence between the four of us. "People make all kinds of assumptions about you. About your family, about your mother. All because you're poor. You're not smart enough, too lazy... and where's your dad, anyways? Maybe he's no good. Maybe he took off because your mom's no good. I just want all of this to be over. I want to be secure financially. Is that such a crime?"

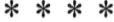

Trish Grady

"There are other ways to make it in life," I pointed out. "How about going back to school? Get an education that will help you land a better job. You'd never make enough as a cashier."

"Unless I married a banker. Maybe even a loans officer," Corinne said sarcastically.

I knew what she was thinking. Who was I to talk? I had relied on my husband's income for over a decade. And I hated myself for it. It's what made me stay all this time. I had become dependent on him.

"Look, with no funds, college was just out of the question," Corinne said now, still quite defensive.

"What about getting a student loan?" Jeremy suggested.

"No." She shook her head. "I'd rather be poor than in debt."

"But that's really short-term thinking," I objected. "Because once you graduate and have a degree, you might land a really high paying job. Then you wouldn't be in debt for long." I couldn't picture my own kids not attending college. Even if we were broke, I'd find a way for them to get an education. Nobody would take that from me.

"What about your mother?" I asked. "Can't she help you out?"

"Leave my mother out of this," she spat out.

"I'm just saying... don't you have any family that can pitch in? What about that aunt you were living with?"

"She's... she's done enough." The aunt was obviously a sensitive subject, and I decided not to push it further. This time it was Jeremy who wouldn't let up.

"Is your mom still living with her?"

"Yes."

"For free?"

"What difference does it make?"

"Who's paying for your mom's expenses?" he persisted.

She stood. "That is none of your business. You have no right...you can ask about me all you want, but don't drag my family into this. This interview is over."

* * * *

Jeremy Lawren

I hadn't expected her to leave. We were all startled. As disastrous as all the previous interviews had been, none of them had ever gotten up and left. Maybe there really was more to these stories, as Rob had claimed. Obviously just a matter of pushing the right buttons.

"What now?" Trish looked at me helplessly.

"Just leave her alone," Stephen said from the stairs, and I wondered how long he had been sitting there.

"I didn't do anything wrong," Trish obviously felt the need to clarify. "Not my fault she's so touchy about that aunt."

"Corinne is supporting her mom," Stephen said. "There, happy now? She can't go to college 'cause she has to support her mom. The aunt's not doing it for free, you know."

"What's wrong with her mom? Why can't she work?"

"She's depressed," Stephen said rather matter-of-factly, as if he'd been a friend of the family his whole life.

"She told you?" Why him? Why not me? After all, I was the director.

"Yes, she told me," he said curtly. "And no, that doesn't make us a couple."

"Who says you're a couple?" Hail wanted to know. I hadn't told him that part. Mainly because I didn't think they were a couple.

"Trish does." Stephen tried to brush it off.

"Why?"

"'Cause she watches too much TV!"

"At least I have watched the show we're competing for! None of you deserves to win!"

"I've seen parts of it." Great, Michael was the last person we needed here right now. "Where's Corinne? Are you guys done already?"

"She left," Trish filled him in. "And no, we weren't done."

"She just got up and left? That's rich. You'd think for two hundred grand she'd try a bit harder. How unprofessional."

"Says who? Your lawyer or your partner-in-business-failure, Julian?" Stephen threw him a hostile look. "Don't you need to consult with them before you make a derogative statement here?"

146

"At least I had the guts to start my own business. You have a crappy job stocking supplies!" Michael looked daggers at him. "Any high school kid can replace you!" he sneered.

"I have my own business. I renovate homes. I don't just stock supplies, I also know how to use them. Which I doubt you do. Ever fixed anything? Oh wait, you couldn't even fix your marriage."

Hail threw me an exasperated look. I didn't feel too sorry for him. I had told him about that part. And then, when I thought things couldn't get worse, Trish burst into tears.

* * * *

Michael Palmer

A while ago I would have dismissed Trish as a drama queen. But she was being sincere. I took a while to learn that, not being an overly emotional guy myself. Which, I now realize, sometimes works against me. People assume I'm callous—which, I can assure you, I'm not. It hit me hard when I realized even Karen had thought that. All those fights, all those times she'd insisted I didn't care. Arguing that I loved her and only wanted the best for her dad got me nowhere. She never believed me. Neither did the jury. Or my lawyer. I got off on a pure technicality. And it never stopped bothering me.

Maybe that's why I chose to believe Trish now. I chose to believe she was being sincere. Things were getting to be too much for her. The constant fighting, having our every move watched and judged, being away from her kids. All that, and the murder nobody wanted to talk about.

Maybe it would have gotten to me too, had I not been through all this before. But I had learned not to yield to emotions. This would just be one more round.

That's why I talked to Julian a lot. He was my sounding board. I could tell him about my dismal shooting days with this dire cast, and he always had an open ear.

"So, she just walked out?" He sounded surprised. "Isn't that the one who really needs the money?"

"Yep, that's her. But honestly, I can't say I blame her." I sighed. "You have no idea what it's like here. I think the producers are just waiting for us to crack."

"I know it's hard. But hang in there." Julian sounded concerned. "Just don't give them the satisfaction. And remember, be careful. Don't volunteer too much info. They're just waiting to make you look bad. It gets their ratings up."

"Right." Ratings, of course. That's all they cared about. How could I have been so stupid? I had come here to restore my life, and instead had landed in this looney bin with a bunch of social outcasts. Way to go.

* * * *

Corinne Prichett

Maybe I was naïve to think they would never ask about her. My mother had problems. I had told Stephen about it, mainly because I was sure he would never bring it up. And I had never told him the full extent of it. It took me a while to understand the full extent of it myself.

When I came home from school, she would be lying on the couch, sobbing into the sofa cushions. I'd assumed she missed Dad. For a while we all did. It would pass, right?

Then my older sister Claudia explained it to me one day. Mom was sick. Really, that was why we were living with Aunt Joan. And here I thought we were just poor.

Mom was on disability. Maybe we could have afforded a place of our own, who knows. But it wasn't an option. Since she couldn't take care of us, Children's Aid would step in. They would remove my sister and me. And so we all remained prisoners in Aunt Joan's little shack. I took the first paying job I found and got out. Claudia got married when she turned twenty-one. She had only dated Andy for a few months. A nice enough guy, but hardly more than her meal ticket. Enough to get out. I once asked Stephen if he had married Irene just to get out. He seemed offended at the time. I just thought it seemed like a good enough reason. But when we left, things didn't change like I thought they would. You cannot escape the responsibility. She was still our mother. And Aunt Joan was no dummy. She knew Claudia and I were now making some money, though I doubt she understood how little. So a short time after, she started insisting Mom had to be watched around the clock now. She had to pay a neighbor to help her when she needed to go out. Her costs were going up. Therefore, so were ours. Our freedom came at a price.

No, I wasn't just trying to win for myself. I'm not that greedy. Or lazy. But I'd rather let the others think that.

* * * *

Trish Grady

Stephen was told to go after her. She obviously wasn't going to listen to Jeremy or me at this point. And Michael... well, the two had never gotten along. I was surprised Jamie had immediately offered his help. That was very considerate of him. But Jeremy didn't seem too pleased. He insisted Stephen go after her instead. Let the secret boyfriend deal with it. Which, of course, meant there would be no more interviews that night.

I was a little embarrassed I had cried in front of them. My nerves, I guess. I retreated to my room in search of some solitude. Funny, I had always considered myself a rather social person. But now I wasn't so sure. With the kids at school and Bill at work, I got used to being home alone. Days were long back then. I wouldn't have minded some company. My life had been pretty boring. But that seemed like such a long time ago. Now alone time felt precious.

This huge house always left me a bit ill at ease. Were we being watched? Were there cameras in our bedrooms, cameras we didn't know about? I remember bringing it up once to the others. But Michael had assured me putting a camera in someone's bedroom was illegal. And Stephen joked that since we had already destroyed two, they weren't gonna waste any hidden ones on us.

I flipped to the paper I'd started reading that morning. Right to the obituary section. I couldn't believe that, after all this time, still nobody had bothered to put out a final notice for Rob. But I had stopped checking when the others were around. They all thought I was being morbid. But my fascination with obituaries didn't originate from any obsession with death. Quite the opposite. I was interested in life. I wanted to know what the sum of it was. What would people say? What would people say about me?

Stephen ruined it a bit for me. He said I couldn't go by that. The funeral homes put the obits together. They were nothing but standard forms, and people just filled in the blanks. Loved and cherished mother/grandmother/aunt of... predeceased by..., her husband of... years. Silly me. I'd always assumed somebody put some thought into these final farewells. Maybe that's why there wasn't one for Rob. There simply was no standard form for murder.

* * * *

Stephen Dowell

Michael was now scheduled to interview me the next day. I wasn't dreading it. I think Jeremy was more nervous about it than me. Not that one could blame him. The poor kid had already lost two cameras. Freaky about that second one though. Still no idea who did that. It wasn't me. Let Michael have his interview, I didn't care. In the end, he could say nothing about me that I didn't already know. He could make me out to be the worst husband on the planet. But it wouldn't be news, really.

What was a little unfair, maybe, was that I had never told Michael I believed he was innocent. I had my fun, watching him squirm. Still having to prove himself to us took him down a couple of notches. And yes, I enjoyed that. But looking back, I probably should have told him.

Corinne and I didn't talk about her mother or aunt anymore, though I think I was supposed to. We just went for a walk, relieved to be out of the house for a while. I told her our time here was almost over. The producers would make a decision about the winner soon. And then we could all get back home. Just hang in there.

I honestly thought the worst was behind us. Man, was I wrong.

Jeremy Lawren

Jamie went back in to work that night. I knew he wanted to run some further background checks on Corinne's family. He pretended to pick up another shift at the photo lab, seeing he was no longer needed for the night. The last of the interviews would start bright and early in the morning, he announced a little too cheerfully.

I was itching to get this over with. Let's face it, none of these guys had killed Rob. The worst they were guilty of was putting out a bad reality show. Couldn't we just slug out this one last round and call it a day?

I was therefore furious when Jamie didn't show up in the morning. What happened to "bright and early"? We were sitting around the patio table. Trish brought up that stupid fire-resistant table top for the umpteenth time. I was on my third cup of a disgustingly weak pot of coffee. Hail had left me with no good excuse for his absence. There were no photo shop emergencies. Why hadn't he at least called in? I alternately stared at my watch and the ominous dark clouds that were starting to move in. We were sure to get some rain.

"Maybe he overslept." Stephen didn't seem terribly concerned.

"I thought he was supposed to sleep here," Trish replied. That's what I had thought, too. Did he get held up at the station? Had he actually found something? I concocted some story about him living somewhere near that fictitious photo lab. So there was a fictitious chance he might have gone straight home from there.

"Have you tried calling him?" Michael asked. I had. Four or five times I had tried to reach him on his cell. Of course I didn't know his home number. I had no idea where Hail lived.

"Have you tried at the photo store?" Corinne suggested.

"Of course," I lied. "He wasn't there anymore. But they have different shifts, and the guy I talked to couldn't even say when he left."

"So, how long are we going to wait for him?" Corinne wanted to know.

"We'll have to wait for him. Remember, he's got the camera."

"Oh, right."

"Let me call Garth, see if he's heard anything." With that I ran up to my room. I would have to check with Hail's police department. Maybe he was still there. He should have called, I thought angrily. How much longer were the others going to buy that photo lab story? What if someone—probably Michael—suggested driving by there? I wasn't an actor, you know. I was the hired help on a crappy soap, recently promoted to sucky director. But actor was not within my brief, okay?

I punched in the familiar number.

"I'd like to talk to Detective Hail. Jamie Hail, please."

"I'm afraid he is not on duty today, sir. Anything I can help you with?"

"Ehm, put me through to his supervisor, please. And could you tell him it's urgent?"

It took a few moments before they connected me. Wonder what their definition of "urgent" was. Maybe Hail was on his way, I kept telling myself.

"Detective Hutchess speaking. How can I help you?"

I briefly explained who I was and that Hail hadn't shown up this morning (all the while keeping my voice down). I kept casting glances at the door, worried about the others lurking in front of my room.

"I will try to get in touch with Detective Hail," Hutchess, who I had no recollection of ever meeting, assured me. "In the meantime, let me know if he shows up or if you hear anything."

"What should I say to the others?" I asked, probably sounding quite desperate at this point. "They're gonna wonder where he is."

"Tell them he got called to the *Crystal Falls* set. Make up some kind of technical trouble, in case anyone asks. And the set is temporarily shut down, so you can't go there." Well, I wouldn't need that excuse. I was reasonably sure nobody wanted to go there.

I hung up, and immediately went for the door. Nobody was behind it. My heartbeat slowed a bit. I could hear them downstairs. They had moved inside to the dining room table. Maybe it had started to rain already. I suddenly felt more discouraged than ever.

* * * *

154

Trish Grady

I should have known this would be a horrific day. It had already come off to a bad start. Jamie was a no-show. The tension in the house was mounting, and there was just a bad feeling in the air. Even the sky had turned awfully dark. Any minute we would see a tremendous downpour.

"Any news?" Stephen asked when Jeremy finally came back down the stairs.

"No, unfortunately nothing."

"So you talked to Garth?" Michael wanted to know.

"I tried to. I couldn't get through to him. They had some problems on the set, that's all I know."

"So we still have no idea where Jamie is?" Corinne summed it up.

Jeremy sighed. "No. I just talked to one of the camera ops. He said Garth was 'indisposed'—which probably means nothing good. He had no idea if Jamie was around. But he said he hadn't seen him."

"So what now, we'll just have to sit here and wait?" I asked.

"Where else would you go?" Corinne snapped at me. "Especially in this weather?"

Some lightning struck in the distance. What would happen should it move closer? It could eventually hit our house. The place sure was a big enough target. Great, that's the last thing I needed. To be sitting here in the dark with four angry roommates. Ironically, that's what we had been doing all along. Just sitting here in the dark. We didn't know who the winner was, or if the producers had already made a decision. I didn't even know who was in charge anymore. I was pretty sure it wasn't Jeremy. Or maybe he did get to give some input, who knows. But Garth? He hadn't displayed an ounce of interest in us thus far, and was clearly overwhelmed as it was. So who exactly were these mystery people going over our tapes?

I tried to distract myself with the daily Sudoko. Corinne and Stephen attempted a game of chess with Michael hovering over their shoulders. He pretended he wasn't watching, but groaned over their every move. Control freak. I hoped Stephen would let him have it in the interview.

It was going on two o'clock, and Jamie was nowhere to be found. I was wondering if he had just skipped town. I used to think that quite a bit about Bill when he was late. Maybe he skipped town. In my mind I'd map out how much time I would give him before I started making calls. Check with his friends, maybe his parents. Start phoning the surrounding hospitals. Between that and my obsession with obituaries, maybe I was a bit morbid. What would I have said about Bill in his obit?

Beloved husband and father… No, I would have left out the "beloved," even back then. But according to Stephen, you didn't get that much input. You just filled in the blanks. Right.

* * * *

Corinne Prichett

Somewhere along the way I stopped believing Jamie would show. If he had at least left us with the camera, we could have just done the interviews without him. He really wasn't that important to the whole thing.

Trish and I were watching TV. Flicking through the channels, really. Stephen had beaten Michael in a game of chess. And poor old Michael was about to lose the rematch, too. He was getting awfully quiet. Just how many times did he have to lose at something to get off his high horse?

Jeremy had stopped leaving messages on Jamie's machine. I guess he figured after four or five of those he'd get the drift: we were waiting for him.

In a couple of days our stay here would all be over. Two initial weeks, plus the two additional ones after the murder. It would finally come to an end. What a waste. Especially those last couple of weeks. First they had told us they required us here for the ongoing police investigation. But then nobody bothered with us after that. Only once had we been called to the station, right after Rob's body had been discovered. We had given our statements and then—boom—nothing. And how could we have been of any help? None of us had even gotten to know Rob. At least not long enough to learn about his friends and enemies. And we weren't anywhere near the crime scene that night. What a colossal waste of time. Was anyone even reading our logs?

* * * *

Stephen Dowell

Michael was a lousy chess player. I guess guys like him inevitably are. He suffered from complete tunnel vision, only ever thinking about the next move. Never considering the grand picture. He had to make his point right then and there without adding up the total. Even after losing everything, he still hadn't changed. Not one bit.

Just think about it for a minute. Maybe his wife really did fall off that balcony in a cruel, accidental twist. I actually thought he had enough evidence on his side. The VISA receipt provided at least some paper trail that he had been at the restaurant. Plus, that job offer had to count for something, right? But he still couldn't convince anyone he didn't do it. I doubt the police ever conducted a thorough investigation. Not with someone looking that guilty right from the start. And the coroner's concession of the possibility of an accidental death probably came through gritted teeth.

See, that's where I felt a bit sorry for him. He couldn't convince police, judge, or jury. And now he was relying on this ridiculous little soap to endear his character to a nation-wide audience? No actor could pull that off, no matter how many Oscars they had under their belt. And I can assure you there were no Oscar contenders on that *Crystal Falls* set.

In a couple of days we would be outta here. I could hardly wait. If I won, Irene would be on TV. Big deal. It wouldn't be her, anyway. But she probably wouldn't have cared if someone else played her. Yeah, she would have gotten a laugh out of it. Finally made me watch her favorite show. And she'd claim it was the sweetest thing I'd ever done for her. And I still felt like crap. I hadn't done anything for her. Well, I had refrained from smashing Michael's teeth in. I should get a gold star for that.

* * * *

Michael Palmer

Something wasn't right. Jamie's suspicious absence was making me increasingly nervous. Of course I couldn't focus on that stupid chess game. Stephen didn't seem to care. At times, I was envious of guys like him. People who—how to say it politely?—didn't seem to put too much thought into things. People who don't fret too much don't go through life expecting the worst. Well, maybe they just haven't gone through enough. True, Stephen—like me—had lost his wife. But he had somehow managed to move on. Rather quickly, if I may say.

Did the others feel uneasy too? Trish always seemed a bit agitated. And Jeremy was nervous. Though I couldn't tell if he was concerned about Jamie's absence or the production deadline he was fast approaching.

Maybe we were all dreading the decision. The results would soon be in, and only one of us would get that coveted spot. Not to mention the money.

I would have liked to believe this experience had at least been some kind of a learning curve for me. That I had taken away something. Be it in the form of TV production experience or maybe even something I had learned about myself. My expectations seemed ridiculous now. For a while I had honestly thought I could learn from the other contestants. People who, like me, had been through tough times and coped. But here's what was fundamentally wrong with our dysfunctional little group: none of us had coped. This show was just supposed to be a quick fix. For Corinne it was nothing but a cash grab. She might as well have played Instant Bingo. Stephen was trying to soothe a guilty conscience by showing his late wife some last-ditch effort. And Trish was aiming to be someone in the eyes of her kids and the friends she never had. But with the exception of giving Corinne a financial boost, this show couldn't help any of us.

* * * *

Jeremy Lawren

By the end of the day, I was resigned to several things. The LA police department would always leave me in the dark. Jamie wasn't coming back. My job here was of absolutely no value to anyone. And we would never solve Rob's murder. Strangely enough, only one of those would prove true. I was mad at Jamie; actually, at his entire police department. They had played me. They never believed the key to Rob's murder was in the contestants. If they did, they would not have left me here on my own. How could I have been so dumb? They were just humoring me. Sure, let the kid hang around them for a while. Maybe he hears something. If the cops had truly believed any of them to be suspects, they would have sent in someone undercover long ago. Instead, they had waited 'til the very last minute. And now the guy wouldn't even bother coming back. And why would he? It was pointless. The cops had read the entries just like I had. There really was no "bombshell" here.

Around seven we finally lost power. The rain beat hard onto the skylights. At times it sounded like a gust of little pebbles, threatening to break the glass. None of us had had the foresight to prepare any candles though Stephen, of course, was quick to find his lighter.

"Does no one know where the breaker box is?" Trish asked, her voice trembling in the dark.

"It's got to be in the electrical room," Corinne replied. "But that's locked."

"You want me to break it open?" Stephen immediately volunteered.

"No," Michael and I replied simultaneously. Upon Michael's suggestion we kindled the neatly stacked logs in the fireplace. I remember fervently hoping it was a functional one, not some sort of prop. Garth would never forgive us.

"So who do you think will win this?" Trish asked when we were gathered around the fire. I could feel her staring at me. "Do you know if they have chosen a winner yet?"

I shook my head. "I have no idea. Though I would assume they'd want to look at the last couple of interviews."

"So what happens if Jamie doesn't show?" Michael asked pessimistically. "I mean, let's face it. It doesn't look like he's going to come. And we're running out of time."

He would be furious if he didn't get to grill Stephen.

"I don't know, we'll have to see. I'd have to get another camera," I said evasively.

"That's just great." Michael was angry now. "We won't have time to organize another camera, you know that. Come on, just tell us straight out. Have they made a decision?"

"I... I really don't know. I assumed they were going to wait 'til the end." I doubted anyone believed me at this point.

"Are you saying someone is actually watching all those tapes?" Trish asked.

"Of course they are." Come on, I thought angrily. One of you guys knows there aren't any tapes. Give yourself up already.

"You're just sore you didn't get to chew out Stephen," Corinne told Michael. "For you, that alone would have been worth the trip, admit it."

"You know what? At this point nothing—apart from the two hundred grand—would be able to compensate me. There you have it. It's really just about the money. Happy now?"

"What happened to clearing your name?" Corinne said mockingly. "Not so important after all?"

"Like that's possible," Stephen scoffed.

Trish gasped. "Are you saying Michael killed his wife?"

"Unlike you, jerk, I cared for my wife," Michael snapped back at him. "You think getting her a part on this crappy show is somehow going to make up for the way you let her down? You got some nerve."

"Hey, you thought this 'crappy show' was good enough to clear your name," I couldn't resist pointing out.

"Yeah, well, I'm certainly cured of that belief."

"So, does that mean you'll drop out?" Corinne asked hopefully.

"You wish. No, I'll stay in. Just to spite you."

"I think you should drop out," Trish sided with Corinne. "You already know you're not gonna get what you came here for. So at least let the rest of us have a shot at it."

Michael looked at her like she had completely lost it. He appeared even more menacing with only one side of his face lit by the fireplace. He would never have allowed us to film him that way.

"You still don't get it, do you?" He stared at Trish, then at the rest of us. "None of you is gonna get what you came here for. It's time you all face that. Trish, your kids are always going to hate you. And you'll still have no friends. Stephen is still gonna be a jerk. And Corinne will forever be remembered as the gold digger who kept someone else's gold. Oh yeah, all that, and Jeremy will still have a crappy job."

We should have left it at that. But here we were, tired, irritated, and offended, forced around the only light source in the house.

Stephen sprang up. "I'm gonna check on those breakers." He certainly had enough pent-up rage to get that door open.

"Look, let's not damage the property," I cautioned, fearing Garth's reaction to any further insurance claims.

"Try and stop me." Stephen made his way down the stairs with nothing but the lighter in his hand. I stumbled after him in the dark.

When we reached the electrical door, he passed the lighter on to me. "Here, hold this." Before I could answer, he kicked the door like the big bad wolf trying to bring down the house. And here was I, his accomplice, shining the light.

"Stephen, stop," I pleaded to no avail.

"We're gonna get sued," Michael's voice came from the stairs.

"Give us some light so no one falls into the pool," Corinne yelled.

I left Stephen kicking against the door and guided the others over.

"What are you trying to do?" Trish panted. "Stephen, stop! I'm not gonna pay for that door!"

"Quit acting like a high school dropout," Michael agreed. "Vandalizing the place isn't gonna help. Take a moment to think, for once."

"Oh, that's rich, coming from you," Stephen sneered back. "If one person here never stopped to think, it's you. You waltz in here, telling everybody how to run their lives. And really, nobody's screwed up more than you. You're probably still wondering who killed your wife!"

"You mean he's like OJ, looking for the real killer?" Trish asked breathlessly.

"I did not kill my wife!" Michael yelled at the top of his voice now.

"I know that, believe it or not," Stephen shouted back at him. "But you still screwed up, big time! You really know nothing about people! Nothing! Right off the start you looked so guilty, I bet the cops never even bothered with anyone else."

"My wife fell off the balcony. It was an accident!"

"You don't even believe that!"

"Then tell me, who killed my wife?" Michael was losing it now.

"Okay," Stephen retorted, "you tell me. You wait for years for your father-in-law to get out of your life. And—boom!—right after your wife dies, he's gone too. How utterly convenient!"

"I don't understand. I didn't kill my father-in-law. I stood nothing to gain from this."

"No, you didn't. Ever wonder where your buddy Julian is getting all his money from? You said he hasn't worked since Karen died. So, I'm asking you, what's he living off?"

I could hear Trish gasp for air. "He didn't want to share the inheritance. That's why he finished Karen off first."

"Finally somebody's catching on."

"You don't know Julian." Michael's voice was shaky now. "He cared very much for his dad and his sister."

"And that's why he carted the old man off somewhere where your wife couldn't keep an eye on him?" Corinne asked coldly.

"Look, this is all speculation." Michael tried to regain his composure. "Even if Julian did do it, there is absolutely no proof."

"I bet Rob found some," I heard myself say. That was it, the bombshell Rob had somehow uncovered! For once in his life he had been right. Unfortunately, it hadn't done him any good.

"Did you tell the police about this?" Trish asked nervously.

"The police? What police? They don't even wanna hear from us about Rob's murder." Stephen kicked at the electrical door again. I should have stopped him right there. When all your instincts tell you something is a bad idea, it's sometimes just that. Stephen was about to kick that door to shreds. I imagined him puncturing a hole into in, somewhere right in the middle. Then, all of a sudden, it completely gave. He was right; it did open to the inside. I came up

beside him, the lighter in my hand, and found myself staring into a
.38.

* * * *

Corinne Prichett

I could barely make out anything; the basement was just too dark. And I'm not just saying that to get out of making a statement. I heard a shot and saw either Jeremy or Stephen go down. A fight broke out somewhere near the electrical room. I panicked. More hitting, punching, grunting. I was afraid the gun could go off at any time again. I ducked for cover behind one of the lawn chairs, half-wondering if that was enough to stop a bullet.

"Intruder!" I heard Stephen yell. Jeremy must have been the one hit.

The gun went off several more times. How many bullets did that thing hold? Maybe we could all just wait and hide until it was empty. I felt bad for Stephen, who was out there by himself, trying to subdue the intruder. He was aiming to push him into the pool, I think. Then I saw the outline of a third person—it had to be Michael. He joined them, and I heard a loud metallic thud.

* * * *

Stephen Dowell

The irony of it all, Michael whacking the guy with the fire extinguisher, hit me much later. The attacker slumped down. At that moment I didn't know if he was dead or alive, and I didn't care. Before we could do anything, we needed light.

I ran to the electrical room and groped for the breaker box. I flicked several switches; nothing. Of course not. When we came down, we hadn't turned on the lights! "Somebody hit the light switch," I yelled. And then I saw Jeremy laying in a pool of blood.

* * * *

Trish Grady

"Call 911!" Stephen hovered over Jeremy, probably checking for a pulse. Corinne made a mad dash for the phone while I just stood there frozen. It all seemed like such a déjà vu with someone yelling for an ambulance and me just standing there. Unable to do anything.

I stared at the second motionless figure on the ground, the guy lying at Michael's feet. I could only see the back of his head. But I found it hard to care about him at that point. The faceless intruder who, a moment ago, had been trying to kill us.

"Ju-... Julian," Michael stammered in disbelief. Of course it was Julian. Silly me, why had I even wondered? He was there to stop us from filming. Just in case Michael won, and the police reopened the case. Right. And Michael had just whacked him with the fire extinguisher. Oh no, not that one again. I panicked. Would Michael have to go back to jail now? It took me a while to process this, probably longer than it should have. But my brain wasn't working well under shock. No, nonsense. This was clearly self-defense. And Michael had plenty of witnesses this time. Phew.

Corinne Prichett

I hung up the phone when the doorbell rang. The ambulance was already here! Had I even told them the intruder was down, too? I honestly couldn't remember. I ran and opened the door, but faced two cops. No sign of any medics.

"Did you bring a stretcher?" I asked breathlessly. The officers looked a little confused. Maybe I did tell them about the intruder, after all. And now they were here to arrest the guy. But they would still need a stretcher for that.

"Miss?" The older one of them looked at me questioningly. "We came to talk to Jeremy Lawren. Is he in?"

"He's hurt. He needs to get to the hospital," I shouted. Hurt? I didn't even know if he was still alive. And what could they want from him? What could possibly be more important than our shooting right now?

At that moment two ambulances pulled up, and a couple of paramedics ran up to the house.

"They're in the basement," I yelled, exhausted, and watched them head down. Then I sank onto the floor and cried.

* * * *

Stephen Dowell

I thought I'd felt a faint pulse. But I have no medical background and wasn't sure if that really meant anything. Jeremy could die from internal bleeding. The hole in his ribcage certainly looked bad enough. And I'd been standing there, right in front of the intruder. He should have shot me. But Jeremy was holding the light, and that's all he saw.

Corinne, Trish, Michael, and I were taken to the police station. 'Cause, suddenly, they wanted to hear from us. Too little, too late. Jamie, whose full name and title, as we learned, was Detective Jamie Hail, had been in a horrific car crash. Someone had cut his breaks.

We couldn't go back to the mansion. And really, none of us would have wanted to. They put us up at the Comfort Inn. But not even The Ritz could have provided anything close to comfort that night. I tossed and turned, my eyes heavy, but my insides churning. I worried about both Jeremy and the undercover cop. Not so much about this Julian guy. Though I did want him to live. He had to live. Someone needed to pay for this.

And I was furious at Michael. He came here to clear his name. Right, nice thought. But, like everything else he did, he was only thinking about that one next move. How hard was it to think this through? If he didn't kill his wife, someone had to. But that moron just waltzed in here, murderer in tow. And we all had to deal with the consequences. Rob dead already and two more lives in the balance. Three, if you counted the murderer. Great. And all because Michael had to make a point.

* * * *

169

Trish Grady

We spent hours at the hospital, mostly hanging around the lobby because they wouldn't let us see Jeremy. He remained in the ICU, and it was touch and go. Poor Jeremy. Always the peacemaker. He didn't deserve to get hurt. I know it weighed heavily on Stephen. He'd gotten the poor boy to hold the light for him. And if he hadn't kicked in that door... Creepy how Julian was often right there with us. Hadn't I always felt like someone was watching me? If I ever came into money, I would never get a big house like that.

The doctors finally gave us an update. They had managed to stop the bleeding, but weren't able to take the bullet out. Jeremy would have to live with it for the rest of his life. Should he live.

After a couple of days his condition was finally upgraded. When I heard the word 'stable', I felt like a hundred pound weight had lifted off me.

I'm sorry to say I could never bring myself to visit Jamie in the hospital. His car accident had been horrendous. They had to cut him out with the jaws of life. As a result, he had lost part of his leg—which one, I don't know. That must have been tough for a young guy like him. Especially one who liked to bike. Yes, I know I probably should have gone to see him. But I had visited a guy who couldn't walk anymore once, and it had been rather traumatic. So sorry, Jamie. Maybe I can write to you one day.

* * * *

Michael Palmer

I was the last to get up when the nurse informed us we could see Jeremy. How could I look the poor kid in the eye? Did he blame me? He had certainly earned that right. They all had. How could I have been so blind? You think you know somebody. I kept going over it in my mind. Julian making the nursing home arrangements—Karen was concerned, why did he have to move him so far away? Julian, who seemed so optimistic about the future, even when our business went down. We'd get back on our feet, right? Julian, the only one who had visited me in jail, unless you count Percara, and he got paid for that.

How could I have been so blind? I had always prided myself for being a man of great foresight. No rash decisions. What an idiot I'd been. The hired help in a warehouse had shown more sense than me. I had never been smart enough, college degree or not. You think after my business failure I would have learned that. And here I was, still full of rash decisions and false judgments. Just look at me: Trish was an annoying, yet boring housewife. Corinne and Jeremy part of the spoiled and lazy youth. And Stephen nothing but a working stiff. And yet, they all had enough class not to shout told-you-so.

* * * *

Jeremy Lawren

It was almost touching. A whole week later, and they were all still here. Considering how much they had wanted to return to their lives, I knew seven additional days were quite a feat. All that just to see me. Just to make sure I'd be okay. The doctors could have told them that much. But here they were, and they had stayed to say goodbye.

Trish rambled on nervously about not having helped out more in the chaos after the shooting. But while she and Stephen attempted apologies, Michael still couldn't bring himself to that step.

But it was okay now. He didn't have to say it. The remorse was in his eyes. He would work through it in his own time. People have their own time, you know. There's no point trying to speed things up. You can't watch a movie in fast forward. Just look at me. I had taken three years to figure out I really didn't want to be here. Kudos to those guys; they had known right from the start.

"I'm sorry I got you into this mess," Stephen apologized again. "This was all my fault. If I hadn't asked you to hold the light..."

"You couldn't have known what was behind that door."

But Stephen shook his head.

"No, we had enough clues something was up. With Trish's diary gone, Michael's disk damaged, the camera wrecked... We could've put it together if we'd just taken a moment. Instead we just pointed fingers at each other."

Still, I couldn't blame any of them now. Maybe prejudices had gotten in the way, but who was I to judge? Really, I'd been no better. All those years I'd looked down on Rob... Then they put me in charge, and it turned out I didn't know the first thing about shooting a production. I would have fired myself long ago. Clearly Rob was much better than I ever gave him credit for. And smarter. Somewhere along the lines he had cracked the case the cops couldn't.

Michael kept staring at a picture above my bed, still avoiding my eye. "I wonder how Rob knew," he murmured. I'm sure he was mulling it over, the countless times he had neatly kept Julian up-to-date about every aspect of us living together. Our shoots, our goings in and out... Julian was always informed. Michael had made it so easy for him. The unsuspecting accomplice. "They found Rob's notes," I told him. "In Julian's motel room. Something about your father-in-law's death didn't quite add up. He'd ingested quite a bit of heart medication, and it belonged to some resident down the hall."

Michael nodded. "He had a history of getting into people's things."

"Right. But not this time. Remember, he had caught that virus that was going around at the nursing home. He was far too sick to leave the bed."

"So he couldn't have made it down the hall!"

"Exactly. But the nursing home was doing their best to sweep this under the rug. They were worried it looked like they had overdosed him. They paid your buddy Julian a fair amount to settle out of court. Three other people died from the virus that month. But Julian was the only one that received compensation. Rob must have caught wind of that somehow."

"All this time, you think you know someone," Michael mumbled, more to himself than to anyone in the room. I knew he was beating himself up. Of all people, Stephen, his arch-nemesis, had figured it out. What a slap in the face. Michael had always pegged him as a simpleton. Not true. A liar, yes. Which was probably why he saw through Julian. It took one to know one.

In the end, there was no winner. All four of them had been through enough, and they decided to split the money. For Corinne, it might be a start.

Julian remained on life support. But even if he did recover, would it be enough to clear Michael's name? Sure, Julian would be formally charged. It would make the papers for a while. But would people look at Michael any differently?

We hugged one last time on the way out. I watched them walk down the corridor, that small group of misfits I suddenly felt I had known my entire life. And I was sad, really. So sad I hadn't been able to give any one of them what they came here for.

ABOUT THE AUTHOR

Kirsten Jany was born and raised in Germany, and emigrated to Canada in 1996. She works in television post production as a sound engineer, and resides in Burlington, Ontario with her daughter and four dogs.